The Executioner®

Don Pendleton's

FRONTIER FURY

D0705647

A GOLD EAGLE BOOK FROM

W RLDWIDE®

TORONTO • NEW YORK • LONDON
AMSTERDAM • PARIS • SYDNEY • HAMBURG
STOCKHOLM • ATHENS • TOKYO • MILAN
MADRID • WARSAW • BUDAPEST • AUCKLAND

Recycling programs
for this product may
not exist in your area.

First edition March 2010

ISBN-13: 978-0-373-64376-9

Special thanks and acknowledgment to
Michael Newton for his contribution to this work.

FRONTIER FURY

Printed in U.S.A.

There is justice, but we do not always see it. Discreet, smiling, it is there, at one side, a little behind injustice, which makes a big noise.

—Jules Renard
1864–1910

Justice may be late, but it's still coming. And there will be blood.

—Mack Bolan

THE
MACK BOLAN
LEGEND

Nothing less than a war could have fashioned the destiny of the man called Mack Bolan. Bolan earned the Executioner title in the jungle hell of Vietnam.

But this soldier also wore another name—Sergeant Mercy. He was so tagged because of the compassion he showed to wounded comrades-in-arms and Vietnamese civilians.

Mack Bolan's second tour of duty ended prematurely when he was given emergency leave to return home and bury his family, victims of the Mob. Then he declared a one-man war against the Mafia.

He confronted the Families head-on from coast to coast, and soon a hope of victory began to appear. But Bolan had broken society's every rule. That same society started gunning for this elusive warrior—to no avail.

So Bolan was offered amnesty to work within the system against terrorism. This time, as an employee of Uncle Sam, Bolan became Colonel John Phoenix. With a command center at Stony Man Farm in Virginia, he and his new allies—Able Team and Phoenix Force—waged relentless war on a new adversary: the KGB.

But when his one true love, April Rose, died at the hands of the Soviet terror machine, Bolan severed all ties with Establishment authority.

Now, after a lengthy lone-wolf struggle and much soul-searching, the Executioner has agreed to enter an "arm's-length" alliance with his government once more, reserving the right to pursue personal missions in his Everlasting War.

Prologue

Nangarhar Province, Afghanistan:
November 22, 2001

The Americans were coming—finally.

They had begun their long-distance assault six weeks before—Tomahawk cruise missiles fired from ships in the Arabian Sea; carpet-bombing from their B-1 Lancers, B-2 Spirits and B-52 Superfortresses—while tribal militias paid and organized by the Central Intelligence Agency rallied to attack the Taliban and warriors of The Base. American Marines and Special Forces had been fighting in the streets of Kandahar and Tora Bora, but they had not ventured far into the eastern countryside.

Until today.

Akram Ben Abd al-Bari heard the helicopters prowling over rocky mountaintops and knew that they had come for him. He couldn't tell their model from a distance, but it made no difference. Where once the Soviets had hunted him with Hinds, now the Great Satan searched for him with AH-64 Apaches, Lynx, or Bell AH-1 gunships. They brought bombs and rockets, .50-caliber machine guns, 20 mm cannons, laser sights and infrared devices.

It was all the same.

The Communists had never found him, nor would the Crusaders.

It was time to flee.

Akram Ben Abd al-Bari saw no shame in running from his enemies. They were superior in numbers and technology, awash in money sucked from oil fields in his native homeland, willing to spend billions of their dollars in pursuit of what they loosely termed "justice."

He had imposed justice upon them—or, at least, a fair down payment on the tab they owed to Allah—with a daring strike against *their* homeland. Now, he would retreat and find another place to hide until the next strike was delivered, and then the one after that.

War everlasting, to the bitter end.

Ra'id Ibn Rashad approached him without fear, as an old friend and valued comrade. "It is time," he said.

Al-Bari nodded, sweeping one more glance around the cave that he had occupied since the Americans first struck, back on October 7. He would not miss the bare walls of stone or the floor that always managed to be damp even though they were surrounded by a desert.

He could settle anywhere, command his global army from a hut or an urban high-rise, issue orders from a tent or even bunker buried in the middle of the Gobi Desert, if need be.

Allah was everywhere, and he would have his victory.

"I'm ready," al-Bari said to his oldest and most trusted friend.

"Come, then," Rashad replied. He wore a Soviet assault rifle over one shoulder, offering its twin to al-Bari with his right hand.

Al-Bari took the rifle, smiled and nodded.

More than two decades had elapsed since he'd last fired a shot in anger, and actually killed another human being with his own two hands. The Soviets had left Afghanistan, defeated, during February 1989. Rather than pause and celebrate that victory, al-Bari moved on to face the next challenge as a commander who directed troops and martyrs in pursuit of Islam's enemies.

It struck him that he had existed in a constant state of war since he was twenty-two years old—more than four decades now—and that unless Allah intervened with some apocalyptic stroke against his earthly foes, al-Bari would be fighting on until the day he died.

So be it.

He had known the risks when he began, had understood that there could be no turning back.

Distant explosions marked the point where pilots had discovered targets, either Taliban or innocent civilians. They would find no Afghan regulars to shoot at in the mountains hereabouts.

Vehicles waited on the unpaved mountain road below al-Bari's cave. Their small convoy would hasten to the border, through the same Khyber Pass that Alexander the Great had used to invade the Indus Valley in 326 BC. Even then, it was well-known to traders, fugitives and bandits.

It would serve al-Bari well.

And he would live to fight again.

The infidels in Washington and London who believed that they had heard the last of him were wrong. *Dead* wrong.

Akram Ben Abd al-Bari was not beaten yet.

His war endured.

1

North-West Frontier Province, Pakistan: The Present

Mack Bolan leaned into the rush of icy wind, his gloved hands clutching the frame of the plane's open doorway. Ten thousand feet below him, rivers, trees and hills resembled landmarks on a model-maker's diorama, tiny and remote.

The pilot's voice came to him through a small earpiece. "On my mark—five…four…three…"

He waited, didn't bother with the thumbs-up signal or a parting word, but simply launched himself on "Go!" The lurch of falling was immediately countered as the aircraft's slipstream caught him, whipping him away.

There was a moment during every jump when Bolan felt as if he wasn't falling, but was rather being blown along sideways, and perhaps he'd keep going in that direction until he had learned to fly on his own power, overcoming gravity itself to soar across the landscape like an eagle. Why should he go down, when all that waited for him on the ground was blood and suffering?

That moment always passed, of course, and as the Earth's pull reasserted its command, he started calculating where to land.

He could control it, to a point. The wind and Earth's rotation played a part, of course, but once his parachute had opened, he could use the steering lines and toggle to control his drift and speed, guiding himself toward touchdown at the preselected site.

Wherever *that* was.

In an exhibition jump, the landing zone would be marked off by colored fabric, smoke bombs, lights, or *something*. A covert drop, by contrast, was intended *not* to advertise his landing for the benefit of those he'd come to find—or for the soldiers who, in spite of public statements to the contrary, might very well be guarding Bolan's targets.

From the moment Jack Grimaldi's plane had crossed the border into Pakistani airspace, Bolan had been on the wrong side of the law. He was a trespasser, intent on the commission of assorted felonies which could, if he was captured, land him in a prison cell for life—or, as it seemed more likely, send him to the wall before a firing squad.

What else is new? he asked himself, then concentrated on the landscape drawing closer to him by the moment.

There! That river with the hairpin turn and twin hills standing just off to the east defined his target. He would try to land inside the loop formed by the river, seeming only inches wide from where he hung in space, but something like a quarter mile across at ground level.

With any luck at all, his native contact would be waiting for him there.

And if he wasn't?

In that case, Bolan would go on and do the job alone, somehow.

Granted, it would be impossible to read road signs, and he wouldn't be able to carry on routine conversations, but he had his maps and GPS device, along with all the killing gear he'd requisitioned for the job at hand.

Think positively, Bolan told himself. There's no reason your guy shouldn't be in place, on time.

No reason except being caught, tortured for information, and replaced by shooters who would zero in on Bolan as he floated toward them from on high, the fire-selector switches on their weapons set for full-auto.

But Bolan didn't worry about what *might* be. It was a rule

he had adopted early in his military service, and it had served him well. Fretting over the possibility of failure would accomplish nothing, but it might become a self-fulfilling prophecy.

A glance at the altimeter on Bolan's right wrist told him he had reached two thousand feet. He found the rip cord, clutched it, counting silently until he knew that he had plummeted five hundred more, then gave the brisk, life-saving tug. The chute rose, deploying overhead, and Bolan felt the shoulder, chest and leg straps of his harness cut into his flesh.

Parachutes had come a long way from the mushroom shapes depicted in films such as *Flying Tigers* and *Twelve O'clock High.* They were lozenge-shaped now, more or less, with individual cells, designed for maximum maneuverability. In Bolan's case, the nylon parachute was colored sky-blue, in the hope that any unintended watchers on the ground below might overlook him.

But it wouldn't help if they had been forewarned of his arrival.

Weighted by the weapons, ammunition and explosives that he carried, in addition to his rations and survival gear, the Executioner started to accelerate once more and used the right-hand brake to manage it.

The river with its hairpin loop was more than just a line drawn on the landscape now. Bolan could see the sun glint off its running water. He had to steer well clear of landing in its depths and being swept away.

He was a strong swimmer, but there was only so much muscle could accomplish when the current seized a parachute and dragged a jumper over jagged rocks, through rapids and somersaulting over waterfalls. It took only one solid blow to snap a neck or bring unconsciousness and allow the river to flood a pair of helpless lungs.

One thousand feet, and Bolan saw a vehicle below him. Only one, and there appeared to be a single figure standing on the driver's side.

So far, so good—unless the lookout was reporting back to shooters waiting out of sight.

Bolan would have a chance to fight, if so, but he had no illusions that the odds would favor him in such a circumstance.

He didn't touch the safety on his AK-47, chosen for deniability if he was caught or killed in Pakistan, like all the other gear he carried. At a thousand feet, he still had time.

But it was swiftly running out.

HUSSEIN GORSHANI watched the stranger plunge toward Earth, while the aircraft that had delivered him turned back and hurried toward the sanctuary of Afghanistan. Most of the Pakistan air force's twenty-seven front-line squadrons were deployed along the border shared with India, far to the south and east, so the plane managed to escape without pursuit.

Leaving one of its occupants behind, falling through space.

Gorshani wondered—not for the first time, by any means—if he had lost his mind. Meeting the stranger and assisting him was certainly a crime under his nation's laws. It might not rank as treason, technically, since spokesmen for the government proclaimed themselves allies with the United States in fighting terrorism, but Gorshani knew his private enterprise would not be cheerfully rewarded by the state police or army.

And, once they discovered that he drew a covert paycheck from the CIA, he would most certainly be killed. The best that he could hope for, in that case, would be a clean death without torture, but he realized that notion verged on fantasy.

The state would want to know how long he'd been employed by the Americans, what he had told them, who his contacts were, and where they could be found. And since Gorshani's sense of honor would not let him answer any such questions, naturally, pressure would be applied.

He knew what that meant, and it gave him nightmares.

Gorshani almost missed the parachute, expecting some dramatic color bright against the washed-out sky, but it was blue, and made him strain his eyes. Even when he had spotted it, the soldier slung beneath it still looked like an insect zigzagging through empty air.

Gorshani took his eyes off the stranger long enough to sweep the road behind him and the open landscape to either side. He knew that he hadn't been followed from Gilgit. He'd have seen vehicles trailing him, or helicopters in the air. But he knew there were ways of finding men and tracking them that he did not pretend to understand—from satellites, high-flying aircraft, even with devices planted in his ancient car.

He'd searched the vehicle before leaving his home, of course, but it was always possible that he'd missed something. New technology didn't require a large device, and he possessed none of the scanners that would locate hidden bugs or trackers by their emanations of magnetic energy.

He had a pistol tucked under his belt, beneath his Windbreaker, for self-defense. It was a Czech CZ-75, purchased at one of the province's countless illegal gun markets, along with the AKMS folding-stock rifle concealed in the trunk of his car.

If the army or state police found him, however, the best thing Gorshani could do for himself was to whip out the pistol and fire a 9 mm bullet through his own brain. Spare himself the agony of interrogation that would last days, or even weeks, until the torturers were satisfied that they knew all his smallest secrets.

Or, he could fight to defend the stranger and himself. Try to flee and escape. Depending on the Yankee soldier's skill, they might just have a chance.

Gorshani saw a subtle glint of sunlight on the nylon parachute, but still had trouble making out its shape against the blue background of sky. No doubt, it was designed that way on purpose, and he hoped that any unseen watchers in the neighborhood would likewise be deceived.

There was no trade route through this portion of the North-West Frontier Province, but some peasants brought their goats and sheep to graze along the hills in spring and summer.

None had been in evidence when he made his approach, but still Gorshani watched for them, prepared to warn them off with threats if necessary while his business was accomplished.

Glancing upward, squinting in the sunlight, he supposed the stranger had to be five or six hundred feet above the ground. What would it feel like, falling from the sky like that? he wondered.

Better than plunging from a helicopter during an interrogation, he supposed, a trick the state police had learned from both the CIA and KGB. It was a technique that produced no answers from its chosen subject, but the prisoners who watched one plummet to his death often became quite talkative as a result.

Two hundred feet, Gorshani guessed, and now he could begin to make out details of the stranger: boots, a smudge of face behind goggles, weapons secured by straps and holsters, and he was wearing sand-colored camouflage fatigues.

One man against the State—or two, if Gorshani counted himself.

Of course, he and this stranger weren't really opposing the government based in Islamabad, simply conducting an end run around its two-faced policy of protecting fugitive terrorists while pretending not to know they existed.

It was a policy that shamed Gorshani's government, his nation—and, by extension, himself. As a patriot and loyal Muslim, he had determined to work against that policy through any means at his disposal. And if that put him at odds with certain politicians or their lackeys, then, so be it.

He was not the traitor in this case.

Clenching his fists, hearing his pulse pound in his ears, Gorshani stood and watched the stranger, his new ally, fall to Earth.

"THERE, SIR! To the west! I see it!"

Second Lieutenant Tarik Naseer turned in the direction indicated by his *havildar*—the Pakistan army's equivalent to a sergeant—and saw a speck descending toward the ground. Naseer raised his field glasses to focus on the falling object.

"Yes!" he said, well pleased. "It is a parachute. One man alone."

"We've lost the plane, sir," said Havildar Qasim Zohra.

"No matter," Naseer said. "We'll have the man himself. Before we're finished with him, he will tell us where he came from and whatever else we wish to know."

The second lieutenant turned and shouted to his soldiers—ten of them standing beside their Russian-made BTR-70 armored personnel carrier.

"Forward with me!" he called. "We go to capture an intruder!"

That said, Naseer took his seat in the open Scorpion Jeep. Havildar Zohra took the wheel and put the Jeep in motion, rolling over open ground toward the area where it seemed likely their target would touch down.

Scanning ahead through his binoculars, Naseer saw that a one-man welcoming committee waited for the parachutist, staring up at the descending jumper from the shadow of a dusty old Mahindra Bolero SUV.

The watcher had not seen them yet. Naseer hoped he could close the gap in time to nab the men without a fight, but there was still a river in his path, its only bridge offset a half mile to his right.

Naseer could try to ford the river in his Jeep, trailed by the APC, but either vehicle could easily bog down, perhaps even be swept away if he misjudged the current. He knew that trying to explain that to headquarters would not be good for his career!

Another possibility was to remain on this side of the river and attempt to kill their targets without questioning the men. The BTR-70 had a 7.62 mm machine gun mounted atop its main cabin, and his soldiers carried AK-107 assault rifles.

Their concentrated fire *should* drop both targets, or at least disable the Mahindra SUV, but Naseer would be held responsible if anything went wrong.

And if he simply shot the two men without first interrogating them, how would he then identify the parachutist, much less learn what brought him to the North-West Frontier Province?

No.

If possible, he needed to procure both men alive. Failing in that, at least the jumper had to be captured and interrogated.

That decided, Naseer made his choice.

"The bridge," he told Zohra. "As fast as you can reach it!"

"Yes, sir!"

Zohra never disputed orders, though he might suggest alternatives if he believed Naseer—twelve years his junior, and with only eight months as an officer—had made the wrong decision. In this case, however, it was clear they only had one way to cross the river and approach their targets.

Which, unfortunately, gave the enemy more time to spot them and escape.

But first, the watcher had to meet his comrade, who was still at least two hundred feet from contact with the ground.

Naseer picked up the compact two-way radio that lay between the driver's seat and his, half-swiveled in his seat as he thumbed down the button to transmit, and called out to the APC behind him.

"Lance Naik Shirazi!"

"Yes, sir!" the APC's gunner replied.

"Prepare to fire, at my command. Take no action without direct orders."

"Yes, sir!"

Behind Naseer's Jeep, the young crewman—ranked on par with a lance corporal—rose through a hatch atop the APC's cabin and readied the vehicle's machine gun, clearing its belt, jacking a round into its chamber.

Naseer still hoped he would not have to kill the strangers, but he would disable their SUV if they tried to escape. Short bursts aimed at the tires, perhaps, or at the fuel tank.

Though the risk of blowing up the vehicle existed, bullets rarely started gasoline fires in such cases. It happened much more frequently in films than in real life.

Naseer clenched his fists as Zohra swung the Jeep away from their targets, accelerating toward the bridge that now seemed more distant than before. Each yard they traveled in the opposite direction felt like a concession to the enemy, as if they were retreating, rather than advancing by the only route available.

He mouthed a silent prayer—Don't let them see us—but would Allah hear him and respond? He couldn't help but wonder if such a trivial request, offered in haste, would even concern Him.

Naseer tried again: for Your great glory and the safety of our nation, let us stop them!

Better, but he could not let the matter shift his focus any further from the mission set before him.

It had been a bland, routine patrol in search of rebels, finding none, until Naseer had heard the distant droning of an aircraft far above their heads. It seemed to come from everywhere and nowhere, all at once, like the infuriating whine of a mosquito buzzing past his ear, while he lay hoping merely for a good night's sleep.

Even with his binoculars, the plane proved difficult to locate, flying at an altitude of two miles, maybe higher. When the parachutist separated from it, Naseer barely glimpsed him, and the jumper's terminal velocity—around three feet per second, if Naseer recalled his jump-school training accurately—made the falling object difficult to track through field glasses.

The sky-blue parachute, clearly, had also been selected to fool watchers on the ground. More evidence that Naseer needed to interrogate the jumper.

But he had to catch him, first.

"Faster!" he told Zohra.

"Yes, sir!"

The Jeep surged forward, pressing Naseer back into his seat.

He watched the SUV and hoped its driver would not notice them.

Hoped that they would not be too late.

BOLAN TOUCHED DOWN within fifty feet of the waiting vehicle, flexing his knees without pitching a full shoulder roll. Before his contact had covered half the intervening distance, the Executioner was stripping off the chute's harness, hauling on the suspension lines and reeling in the nylon canopy.

"I'll help you," the Pakistani said, fumbling for a set of lines, snaring them on his second try.

"We ought to bury it," Bolan replied—then glanced across the river toward a pair of speeding military vehicles and added, "But I guess we won't have time."

His contact turned to stare in the direction Bolan faced, and blurted out what sounded like a curse.

"Leave it," Bolan ordered. "We need to go right now."

They dropped the tangled lines, leaving the parachute a plaything of the breeze, and ran back toward the SUV. Bolan was faster, got there first, ignored the shotgun seat and climbed into the rear.

The Pakistani threw himself into the driver's seat and reached for the ignition key as Bolan asked him, "Do you have a weapon?"

Reaching for his hip, where Bolan had observed a pistol's bulge beneath the Windbreaker, the man reconsidered. "Underneath the hatch in back," he said. "A rifle."

Bolan found it, recognized an older model of the AKSM he was carrying and passed it forward. His companion dropped it on the empty shotgun seat and put the SUV in motion, fat tires churning dirt and gravel in their wake as he accelerated from a standing start.

How long before the soldiers reached the bridge, then doubled back along the route to overtake them? Bolan made the calculation in his head and guessed that they had five minutes to put more ground between themselves and their pursuers now, before the race turned into life or death.

Five minutes wasn't much.

He doubted it would be enough.

"Where are we going?" Bolan asked his driver.

"North, eventually. If we are not killed or captured."

"Let's avoid that, all right?"

"I will do my best."

And Bolan wondered whether that was good enough.

His plans hadn't included taking on the Pakistan army—which, with some 700,000 personnel and another half million in reserve, outnumbered that of the United States. However, since the rulers in Islamabad permitted terrorists to hide in Pakistan and operate with virtual impunity from Pakistani soil, he had anticipated opposition from the military.

And he'd come prepared.

Bolan's AKMS assault rifle came equipped with a stubby GP-25 40 mm under-the-barrel grenade launcher, and he carried a variety of munitions to feed it. His 75-round drum magazine gave him extended firepower for the Kalashnikov, backed up for closer work by a Belgian FN Five-seveN semiauto pistol, chambered for the high-powered 5.7 mm cartridge tailored for long range and superior penetration, with a 20-round box magazine and no external safety. His hand grenades were Russian RGD-5s, with 110 grams of TNT and liners scored to fling 350 lethal fragments over a killing radius of sixty feet.

With that gear, and his companion's AKMS rifle, Bolan was up against a light machine gun with a range around 860 yards, and ten or twelve Kalashnikov assault weapons, likely firing 5.56 mm NATO rounds, with an effective range of 650 yards. Put all that hardware together, and his pursuers could lay down a blistering screen of some eleven thousand rounds per minute.

In theory.

In fact, however, none of the APC's soldiers could fire while their vehicle was rolling in hot pursuit. That left the APC's machine gunner and the Jeep's shotgun rider, for a maximum of two weapons engaged, and the APC's weapon had a 210-yard advantage over anything the Jeep's rider was carrying.

Say five hundred rounds per minute for the 7.62 mm MG, and allowing for spoilage of aim, as the eight-wheeled, 11.5-ton BTR-70 pitched and rumbled on its way at top speed, and they might be all right.

Might be.

The safer plan was to remain outside the machine gunner's 860-yard effective range, thus rendering his task that much more difficult, but that was down to Bolan's driver—whom he'd never seen in action previously, and whose vintage SUV was subject to the same foibles as any other man-made vehicle.

Call it a race for life, then.

He was barely on the ground in Pakistan, and Bolan's mission already hung in the balance.

They should be able to outrun the APC, with its factory-standard top speed of fifty miles per hour, but bullets were faster, and that still left the Jeep on their tail.

No matter how well his driver managed to perform, Bolan would have to derail the soldiers in the Jeep—and hope they hadn't radioed ahead for reinforcements to establish road-blocks on the highway leading northward.

One thing at a time, Bolan thought, as he focused on the military vehicles behind him. The Jeep had just crossed the river bridge and was accelerating after them, its shotgun rider hanging on for dear life as his driver put the pedal to the floor.

Another moment and the APC was after them, its turret gunner rocking helplessly behind his MG, still too far away to sight and fire.

How long could Bolan's driver hold that slim advantage? Were his tires in decent shape? Had he maintained his engine? Was the gas tank full?

Too many questions.

Bolan crawled over the SUV's backseat, onto the rear deck in the hatchback section. He would play tail gunner when the enemy closed in behind them.

And with any luck, he just might live to fight another day.

2

Shenandoah National Park, Virginia: Two days earlier

Skyline Drive was aptly named. It ran along the spine of the Blue Ridge Mountains for 105 miles, from Front Royal at the northern terminus to Rockfish Gap at the southern end. Because its full length was within a national park, visitors paid an entry fee of fifteen dollars per car or ten dollars per motorcycle, thus obtaining a seven-day pass.

Mack Bolan could have saved his money by displaying an ID card he'd received from Hal Brognola through a drop box, which identified the bearer—"Michael Belasko," with a nonexistent address and a photo that could pass for Bolan's likeness—as an employee of the National Park Service, but he'd figured why bother?

He didn't need to see the ranger in the ticket booth look worried, wondering if he'd done something wrong, or if something critical was happening inside the park and he had missed the memo.

Anyway, the fifteen bucks made Bolan feel that he was giving something back.

Built between 1931 and 1939, at the nadir of the Great Depression, Skyline Drive was convoluted and tortuous. Scenes of epic beauty dazzled drivers all the way, but caution was required on the winding turns where bicycles and black bears shared the relatively narrow highway. Park police enforced a strict 35 mph speed limit, and Bolan didn't want to risk a speeding rap.

Rolling through Mary Rock Tunnel, 670 feet of pitch darkness, with his headlights on high beams, Bolan wondered where Brognola planned to send him this time. There had been no warning on the telephone—there never was—and Bolan had been left, as usual, to speculate in vain.

One thing he knew beyond a shadow of a doubt—it wouldn't be a social call.

Somewhere, somehow, someone had stepped across a line, and Bolan would be sent to reel them back or punch their ticket for one long, last ride.

He could refuse the job, of course. That flexibility was built in from the start. But in reality, he'd only turned thumbs-down on a few assignments in the time he'd worked with Brognola and the assembled team at Stony Man Farm.

The Farm was named for Stony Man Mountain, the fourth highest in the park at 4,010 feet, but it wasn't actually on the mountain. It did not appear on any map available for public scrutiny, and while it was a working farm—in more ways than one—its crops were not marketed under the Stony Man name.

Trespassing was rigorously—sometimes fatally—discouraged.

Roughly half the time, when Bolan visited the Farm, he flew in and out. Stony Man had its own airstrip and helipads, complete with stinger missiles and hidden batteries of anti-aircraft guns to deal with any drop-ins who ignored the radio commands to steer clear of restricted airspace.

It had only happened once, to Bolan's knowledge, with a careless pilot running short of fuel halfway between Pittsburgh and Winston-Salem. In that case, the guns and rockets hadn't fired, but several days of house arrest and chemically induced amnesia left the interloper scrambling to explain how he had missed his scheduled wedding.

The groom did not live happily ever after with his bride… but at least he lived.

Some others who had trespassed at the Farm with sinister intent were not so fortunate.

Bolan cleared the tunnel and killed his headlights, braking just beyond the next curve for a line of deer crossing the road. A nine-point buck was last across, pausing to stare at Bolan for a moment through the tinted windshield of his rental car.

Bolan wondered if the deer spent their whole lives inside the park's 306 square miles, or if they sometimes strayed outside. With hunting season on the way, he wished them luck.

So many predators, so little time.

BOLAN DIDN'T try to spot the guards staked out along his route of travel from the gate to the farmhouse that served as Stony Man's HQ. He was expected, so went unchallenged by the Farm's team of "blacksuits."

At any given time, Stony Man's security staff included active-duty members of the U.S. military who dressed as farmhands but were armed.

Brognola was waiting on the farmhouse porch with Barbara Price—the Farm's mission controller—when Bolan got there, slowing into his approach. A stocky farmhand with a military buzz cut waited two steps down, to spirit Bolan's rental car away and out of sight once he had cleared the driver's seat.

"Good trip?" Brognola asked, as Bolan climbed the porch steps and shook his hand.

"Normal," Bolan replied.

It was the standard small-talk introduction to his latest job. He hadn't flown across country from San Jose to Washington, then driven south from there to Stony Man, to talk about the Shenandoah scenery.

"Okay," Brognola said. "We may as well get to it, then."

But first, they had to reach the War Room, situated in the

farmhouse basement, theoretically secured against direct hits with conventional munitions. That remained untested, and if all of them were lucky, it would stay that way.

They rode the elevator down and disembarked into a corridor that led them to their destination, through a coded secure access door. Aaron "the Bear" Kurtzman was waiting for them in the War Room. He was seated in the wheelchair that had kept him mobile since a bullet clipped his spinal cord, during an armed assault on Stony Man.

Bolan shook hands with Kurtzman, then moved around the conference table to take a seat to Brognola's left, while Barbara took the right-hand side. Kurtzman remained at the keyboard that controlled the War Room's lights and AV apparatus for events such as the current mission briefing.

"Akram Ben Abd al-Bari." Brognola managed the pronunciation flawlessly, smiling grimly as he said, "You recognize the name, of course."

"It rings a bell," Bolan replied.

Brognola didn't need to tell those present that al-Bari had been among the FBI's Ten Most Wanted fugitives since 2001, with a four million dollar price tag on his head, dead or alive. Although the names on that dishonor roll were not officially prioritized, only al-Bari's boss—known in the trade as O.B.L.—rated a higher bounty. Both had managed to evade manhunters during the Afghanistan invasion and remained at large, with open warrants naming some four thousand murder victims from the 9/11 raids and other terrorist events dating from 1993.

Behind Brognola, Kurtzman displayed revolving photos of al-Bari on the large screen. Like the human monster's reputation, the images were several times larger than life-size. Bolan had seen them all before, including the grainy captures from the latest video that had been aired last month on CNN and BBC, promising hell on Earth for the American Crusaders and their lackeys.

"Also among the missing," Brognola announced, "Ra'id Ibn Rashad, his number two."

More photos appeared on the big wall-mounted screen. Rashad's brown, bearded face was seldom seen on Western television, and while he didn't rank among the Ten Most Wanted, he was close. One million dollars waited for the bounty hunter who could bring him in alive, or prove beyond the shadow of a doubt that he was dead.

Delivering his hands would do it.

Or his head.

"Big fish," Bolan said, "but they're still not in the net—are they?"

"No, you're right," Brognola said. "But now we have a good idea of where to drop our line."

"That sounds familiar."

There'd been countless leads on al-Bari, Rashad, and O.B.L. himself, over the years. One thing the tips all had in common was that none of them had panned out. Agents and mercs had died on some of those wild-goose chases. But most had simply ended in frustration, time and money wasted in pursuit of shadows.

"Sure it does," Brognola said. "Except…"

Another photo came up on the screen. This one revealed al-Bari and Rashad in conversation, over plates of food Bolan couldn't identify. The angle of the shot made him suspect it had been snapped clandestinely.

"That's new?" he asked.

"Taken ten days ago," Brognola said.

"Location?"

"Somewhere in Pakistan's North-West Frontier Province. We don't have exact coordinates."

That stood to reason. If the Pentagon could put their finger on al-Bari and Rashad, they likely would have plastered him with smart bombs and cruise missiles, then apologized to the Islamabad authorities at leisure—if at all.

Bolan could see where this was going.

"Someone has to go in and confirm it," he said, not asking.

"Right. And take whatever action may be feasible, once confirmation is achieved."

"Presumably with someone who can speak the language."

"Absolutely," Brognola agreed.

"Okay," Bolan said. "Let me hear the rest of it."

THE REMAINING DETAILS were quickly delivered. "Someone" had located al-Bari's hidey-hole in northwest Pakistan, where he shared lodgings with Rashad and other members of al Qaeda. Some of them were only passing through—dodging pursuers, picking up their orders or delivering reports—but there appeared to be a constant staff of four or five top aides in residence, plus bodyguards.

How many guards?

No one could say, with any certainty.

After the briefing, Bolan went up to his usual room. Brognola, or someone acting on his orders, had prepared a CD-ROM containing biographical material on Bolan's two main targets and his Pakistani contact, plus a summary of known al Qaeda actions since the group was organized in 1988. Born out of battle with the Soviets in Afghanistan, al Qaeda—"The Base," in Arabic—was a fluid band of Sunni Muslim militants, founded by one Abdullah Yusuf Azzam. A bomb blast killed Azzam and his two sons a year later, in November 1989, outside a mosque in Peshawar. Suspects named in different media reports included the Mossad, the CIA, and O.B.L. himself. Officially, the case remained unsolved.

The rest was history. With O.B.L. in charge, warriors of al Qaeda rolled on to murder thousands, from New York and Washington to London and Madrid, Djerba and Casablanca, Istanbul and Aden, Nairobi and Dar es Salaam, Jakarta and Bali. The world was their battleground. Their stated goals: destruction of Israel, eradication of all foreign influence from Muslim nations, and establishment of a new Islamic caliphate.

In practice, that meant killing anyone who disagreed with them on any point of doctrine, or who was perceived to aid the group's enemies. Bolan had faced al Qaeda members in the past and managed to survive, but this would be his first crack at the group's top-level leadership.

Which brought him to the men themselves.

According to Brognola's file, Akram Ben Abd al-Bari had been born in Cairo, in September 1951. His father was a pharmacist and teacher, from a long line of physicians and scholars active in radical politics. Al-Bari joined the Muslim Brotherhood at age fourteen, went on to study medicine and served in the Egyptian army as a surgeon, married and had two daughters. By 1980 he was rising through the ranks of the Egyptian Islamic Jihad, which merged with al Qaeda in 1998. Three years later, when American smart bombs leveled Taliban headquarters at Gardez, Afghanistan, al-Bari's wife and daughters died in the rubble.

Al-Bari escaped and channeled his grief into rage.

Ra'id Ibn Rashad was another Egyptian, younger than al-Bari. Conflicting CIA reports claimed he was born in April 1960 or November 1963, but neither date was relevant to Bolan. Rashad was a suspect in the 1981 assassination of Egyptian president Anwar Sadat, but he'd dodged indictment in that case and fled to Sudan with other members of al-Bari's Egyptian Islamic Jihad, later following his mentor into a merger with al Qaeda. FBI reports named Rashad as a guiding force behind two U.S. embassy bombings in 1988, which claimed 223 lives in Kenya and Tanzania, leaving another 4,085 wounded. Rashad had missed a spot on the FBI's Ten Most Wanted list, but made the Bureau's roster of Most Wanted Terrorists when that program was created after 9/11.

Neither target was a combat soldier, though Rashad had done his share of training in assorted desert camps. They weren't guerrilla fighters in the normal sense, but both had proved themselves die-hard survivors, living on the run for over a decade, while the combined military and intelligence networks of the United States and Great Britain tried to hunt them down.

That told Bolan that they were determined and had a very strong support system. He wondered, now, if either man suspected that their hideout had been blown. Beyond the knowledge that their deaths obsessed some operatives in Washington and London, did al-Bari or Rashad know that specific plans were in the works to kill them?

Bolan had no way of knowing for certain if Brognola's information was correct, but the team at Stony Man Farm had never let him down before. Yet Bolan knew that every operation was a fluid, living thing.

At least until the final shots were fired.

Al-Bari and Rashad might know they'd been exposed, or they might simply crave a change of scene and slip away before he got to Pakistan. In which case, Bolan might be able to pick up their trail—or he might not.

Some of the burden rested on his native contact, one Hussein Gorshani. Brognola's dossier said that Gorshani would turn thirty-four the following month. He owned a small repair shop in Islamabad, specializing in electronics, and had roughly quadrupled the country's average per capita income of $2,900 over the past ten years. He also drew a modest paycheck from the CIA, which was a story in itself.

Pakistan is a self-proclaimed Islamic republic, and while about ninety-seven percent of its people subscribed to the faith, some Muslims were more equal than others. Hussein Gorshani belonged to the Shia minority, outnumbered four- or five-to-one by hostile Sunnis. Still, Gorshani's dossier claimed that religious persecution had not sparked his decision to work for Langley. Rather, that had come about by slow degrees, as Gorshani observed his nation's leaders drifting ever closer to covert support for O.B.L. and al Qaeda.

Gorshani had served four years in Pakistan's army, rising to the rank of *havildar,* or sergeant. As a native of the North-West Frontier Province, he had served most of his time there, on border patrols with the paramilitary Frontier Corps. He was also trilingual, rated as fluent in Pashto, Urdu and English.

An all-around Renaissance man.

There were, however, two things that Brognola's dossier could not reveal about Hussein Gorshani. First, despite his military training, there was nothing to suggest he'd ever fired a shot in anger at another human being. When the crunch came—and it would—could Bolan trust Gorshani to pull the trigger on one of his own countrymen?

The second question was more basic, but equally vital.

Could Bolan trust Gorshani at all?

Turncoats, double and triple agents were a dime a dozen in the murky realm of cloak-and-dagger operations. Every nation had its clique of spies, and the U.S. had more than most. Each and every spy network on Earth used bribery and blackmail to recruit from opposition groups, as well as from civilian populations.

Who could absolutely guarantee that Bolan's contact wasn't secretly working for Pakistan's Intelligence Bureau, its Federal Investigation Agency, or some military outfit under the umbrella of Islamabad's Directorate for Inter-Services Intelligence?

Answer: no one.

It was a risk that Bolan ran each time he set foot onto foreign soil, relying on a local contact. He had beat the odds so far, but that just meant that he was overdue to roll snake eyes.

Bolan's less-than-comforting thoughts were suddenly interrupted by a cautious rapping on his door.

"OH, GOOD. You're decent," Barbara Price observed, as Bolan stood aside to let her in.

"Depends on who you ask," he said.

"I guess it would." She nodded toward the open laptop with Gorshani's mug shot on the monitor's screen. "We're pretty sure he's clean," she said, as if reading his mind.

"And he's the only game in town," Bolan replied.

"That, too."

"He's not the one who blew the whistle on al-Bari and Rashad, though."

"No," she said, "he's not. Langley won't part with that name. They've supposedly got someone deep on the inside."

"So, he could do the job himself," Bolan suggested.

"That was Hal's first thought, but Langley doesn't want to lose him. After all, someone's bound to replace al-Bari and Rashad after you take them out. As long as Mr. X is still in place, the Company can track al Qaeda's leadership."

"The greater good," Bolan said.

"Right. But I'd still be happier if Langley wasn't in the mix at all."

Some people blamed the CIA for al Qaeda's existence, noting that the Agency had funneled arms to O.B.L. and others in Afghanistan to help them slaughter Russians, back when O.B.L. was still a "patriot" and "friend" of the United States. In fact, some claimed al Qaeda didn't exist at all, but had been fabricated by the CIA to keep those covert dollars pouring in.

"We take what we can get," Bolan replied.

"Speaking of that," she said, and reached for Bolan's hand. But before going any further, Price paused and said, "Listen, this is serious. About Gorshani."

"I know."

"We've checked him out as far as possible, same as we always do—but this is Pakistan."

"Meaning they've elevated subterfuge to art-form status?" Bolan said.

"Meaning it's a bloody can of worms. The North-West Frontier Province makes Medellín look like Utopia. They stopped publishing casualty figures in 2004, when the tally became too embarrassing. And it's not just the government versus rebels. Every village has at least one illegal arms dealer. In the cities, you can't walk a block without tripping over Kalashnikovs and RPGs. They've logged more than twelve thousand arrests for gun-related crimes over the past three years, and that's barely scratching the surface."

"Sounds like Dodge City," Bolan said.

"Dodge City on angel dust," she replied, "with unlimited ammo and a side order of religious fanaticism. On top of which, if you can make it past the bandits and militias, we suspect the government is covering your targets."

"If I didn't know better," he said, "I'd think you wanted me to pull the plug."

"Who says I don't?"

"Sounds to me like a conflict of interest."

"You want it straight? I've been against this from the start, but I was overruled. Okay. I'm a team player. But it stinks."

"A chance to cut the snake's head off," he said. "Or close, at least."

"That's how they're selling it. But why *can't* the Agency's man come up with coordinates for an air strike? You want to tell me he can snap a photo of the targets, but he can't jot down the longitude and latitude? Come on!"

"My guess would be he doesn't want to go up with the others."

"And are you supposed to recognize him, when you get there? What's he gonna do, whip out his CIA decoder ring before you drop the hammer on him? And he'll *still* be working as an asset undercover, after *that?* Somebody's blowing smoke."

"Maybe," Bolan said. "But I can't see through it till I'm on the ground."

"I knew you'd say that," she replied.

"What else can you predict?" he asked.

"A long night for the two of us," she said, and offered Bolan a slow smile as she led him to the bed.

3

North-West Frontier Province, Pakistan: The Present

Fleeing over open ground meant there was nothing to obstruct the enemy's sight line or spoil their aim. All Bolan and his contact had going for them now was speed, and the Executioner hoped his driver was equipped to make the most of it.

Crouched on the SUV's rear deck, Bolan was crowded by a spare tire on his right—the driver's left—but he had room enough to fight. And room enough to die in, if the APC's machine gunner was capable of holding steady on a target at the far end of his killing range.

But not just yet.

The Jeep was Bolan's first concern, though. With only two men inside, and the driver fully occupied with his appointed task, the Executioner had the advantage. At most, the driver might fire pistol shots, but, then again, aiming would be difficult unless he dropped the Jeep's windshield.

That left the passenger, whom Bolan took to be the officer in charge of the patrol. He couldn't read the soldier's face at four hundred yards, much less determine his rank, but the man was holding some kind of rifle, biding his time.

Bolan thought he'd give the lead pursuers something to think about, and began firing from a seated position. With elbows braced on knees, it was the best position next to prone for steady shooting, but that was, of course, from solid ground. Each time his driver swerved or hit a pothole in the pavement, Bolan lurched along with the whole SUV.

His first shot, therefore, may have been a miss. He saw the two Jeep-riders duck their heads, but saw no evidence of impact on their vehicle. The Jeep held steady, barreling along in hot pursuit.

For number two, still set on semiautomatic fire, Bolan aimed at the center of the Jeep's windshield and squeezed the trigger. This time, it was nearly on the mark but high and slightly to the left, missing the rearview mirror by an inch or so.

Still, Bolan got the physical reaction that he'd wanted, smiling as the Jeep swerved wildly for a moment, slowing at the same time, while its driver tried to choose between the gas and brake pedal, guts or survival.

Bolan saw the shotgun rider turn and shout something at his wheelman. Whatever he'd said convinced the driver to accelerate despite incoming fire.

Behind the Jeep, the eight-wheeled APC was giving all it had to stay in the race. Its twin Russian-made ZMZ-49-05 V-8 engines strained to hit and hold the vehicle's top speed, around fifty miles per hour. That was good time for patrolling or advancing on a line of rioters, but in a car chase it was almost bound to lose.

Almost.

Bolan observed the shotgun rider in the Jeep half-standing, lining up a rifle shot over the windshield's upper edge. It wasn't likely he would score the first time out, but there was always the threat of a lucky shot.

Bolan thumbed the fire-selector switch on his AKMS from single shot to 3-round bursts, then braced the black fiberglass-reinforced polyamide snug against his shoulder. A trained shooter brought the weapon to his face, not vice versa, and Bolan was one of the best. But even so, he couldn't abrogate the laws of physics.

His first 3-round burst was aimed at the grille, but went low and outside. Not low enough to shred the left front tire, but knocking shiny divots in the fender just above it.

Correcting for the second try, he saw two rounds ricochet from the Jeep's dusty hood, one scarring the windshield, the other long gone. As for the third round, Bolan couldn't guess where it had wound up.

The chase car's driver swerved again, but brought it back on track this time without a warning from his passenger. The officer had fallen back into his seat when Bolan fired, ducking and covering as best he could while riding in an open vehicle, but now he rose again, aiming his rifle toward the SUV.

It's coming, Bolan thought, and ducked beneath the SUV's tailgate. Between the wind rush and the growling engine of the SUV, Bolan had trouble hearing any shots fired from behind him. He didn't know, therefore, how many times the Pakistani officer had missed before a bullet drilled the tailgate, inches from his sweaty face.

From there, it punched through the backseat, missed Hussein Gorshani's elbow by a whisper and buried itself in the dashboard.

"They're shooting at us!" his driver cried.

Bolan didn't bother answering the obvious. His mind was searching for a way to get the shooters off his back—or send them all to hell.

HUSSEIN GORSHANI cursed in Pashto, gripping the SUV's wheel with a white-knuckled mixture of fury and fear. The soldiers had damaged his car and were trying to kill him. His hatred for them, in that moment, was boundless.

Never mind that he was technically in the wrong, and that they were only doing their jobs. The gunfire was a product of Gorshani fleeing, and his passenger had started it by firing at the Jeep first.

For all the good *that* did.

Evasive driving might have helped, but they were speeding

down a narrow road, poorly maintained, and he was more likely to spoil his ally's aim than the enemy's.

Gorshani had anticipated danger when his CIA contact proposed the operation, but he'd thought they would move toward it gradually, conferring and learning to trust one another before they plunged into hot water.

Now, it seemed, he was at war not only with the hidden leaders of al Qaeda, but also with the soldiers of his homeland.

Traitor, said a small voice in his head.

Gorshani had once been a soldier himself, had ridden in a Talha APC through hostile territory in the North-West Frontier Province of his birth. He had never been in battle—though his APC had twice come under sniper fire. It had been strange, sitting in a metal box, listening to bullets *ping* against the armored sides.

Gorshani wished he had some of that armor now, but knew he'd have to settle for the SUV's superior acceleration. He knew his vehicle could literally drive rings around the BTR-70—not that it would be a wise thing to attempt—and Gorshani was confident he could outrun the Jeep if his tail gunner failed to disable it.

Unless a bullet found him, first.

The near-miss had unnerved him, driving home the point—if any emphasis was needed—that Hussein Gorshani was a mortal man. He could be killed or mutilated by a bullet in a heartbeat, leaving his comrade adrift as the SUV swerved, stalled and died.

Not yet, he thought, and glanced at his rifle on the passenger's seat to his right. If need be, he would stop the car and fight, go out with the American in what was sometimes called a blaze of glory.

Checking his rearview mirror, he could see the nearest chase car gaining ground. The tall American rose and blocked Gorshani's view, squeezed off another burst of automatic fire, then dropped back out of sight.

The Jeep reacted with a wide swing to Gorshani's left, then roared back into line behind his SUV. It seemed unstoppable, a monster in its own right that could not be killed.

Ridiculous!

It was a man-made object, just as vulnerable as Gorshani's car to damage caused by road hazards or bullets. Granted, it had probably been built for driving over worse ground than the SUV, and yet…

An idea flashed into Gorshani's mind. He called out to his crouching passenger, "I want to lead them off the road."

"What for?" the American asked. "The Jeep and APC are built for it."

"The vehicles," Gorshani said, "but maybe not the men."

"Can this rig take it?"

"We shall see."

Just as Gorshani spoke, another rifle bullet struck the SUV a glancing blow and whined off into space. The tall American responded with another 3-round burst and shouted to Gorshani, "Go for it!"

Gorshani gripped the steering wheel, swept anxious eyes along the roadside, left and right, then made his choice. If he chose left, the river would eventually block him. But on his right, the open grassland beckoned.

Done.

He cranked the wheel and stood on the accelerator, slumping in his seat to let his slack body absorb the impact of rough ground beneath his tires and shock absorbers. Ten yards into it, his teeth were clacking and he felt a sudden urge to urinate that almost made him laugh aloud.

I should have gone before the chase, he thought, and then he did laugh.

"What's so funny?" his passenger asked.

"Nothing!" Gorshani answered, as the Bolero slammed into a low ridge of soil and briefly went airborne. Its landing jarred him, nearly making him release the steering wheel. But he hung on and brought the vehicle under control.

A quick glance at the rearview mirror showed the Jeep careening after him, and the APC charging along behind.

SECOND LIEUTENANT Tarik Naseer braced himself—legs rigid, one hand pressed against the Jeep's dashboard, teeth clenched to keep them from snapping together and chipping.

He had fastened his seat belt when they first struck off in pursuit of their targets, then had unlatched it so that he could stand and fire his AKMS over the Jeep's windshield frame. But as the Jeep left the pavement and sped across rough open ground, he regretted that choice.

Naseer had ordered his driver to follow the SUV when it left the roadway, but now he was trapped in his seat—or rather at risk of being thrown from it. He needed one hand braced against the dash to keep from pitching forward and striking his head on the windshield, while his other hand clutched the Kalashnikov. He could not reach his seat belt and secure it without losing one grip or the other, and the options were unacceptable.

"Watch out!" the driver cried just as he hit yet another deep rut in the earth. The Jeep bounced twice before settling, each leap unseating the lieutenant. For an instant his heart was in his throat. He was terrified of being thrown completely from the vehicle.

He wondered if Qasim Zohra would even notice, should his passenger be catapulted into space. The driver was completely focused on his target, leaning forward in his seat as if such posture might increase the Jeep's acceleration.

Naseer considered exactly what could happen if he fell out of the Jeep. Would his neck snap on impact with the ground? If he was pitched over the Jeep's rear deck, somehow, would he be crushed beneath the APC, or could its driver stop in time?

Another vicious jolt, causing Naseer to mouth a curse. The men he was pursuing would have faced enough trouble, had they simply surrendered on the spot. But now…

The driver barked another warning, ducked low in his seat, just as Naseer saw the rear gunner in the SUV rise to fire another burst. Two of the bullets struck the Jeep's windshield this time, spraying Naseer with shards of broken glass.

Enough!

Releasing his grip on the dashboard, Naseer raised his rifle and aimed through the gap in the shattered windshield. Just as he squeezed the trigger, Zohra hit another deep hole with the Jeep and nearly spilled Naseer out of his seat. His burst of autofire was wasted, with the last round clanging off the windshield's upper frame.

A bitter curse escaped his lips, and the second lieutenant swung around toward Zohra, shouting, "At this rate, you will kill us before he does!"

"I'm sorry, sir," Zohra replied. "Shall I slow down?"

Naseer considered it for half a second, glancing back toward the oncoming APC, then said, "Do *not* slow down. But hold the Jeep steady, so I can aim!"

Even as Naseer spoke the words, they seemed ridiculous to him, a feeling mirrored on his driver's face. Zohra could not control the contours of the landscape, any more than he could turn the Jeep into a hovercraft and make it fly.

Another short burst from the SUV came in on target, rattling off the Jeep's curved hood. Naseer ducked, felt a bullet cleave the air beside his face and heard his driver yelp in pain.

"Zohra?"

"It's nothing, sir. A scratch."

Naseer saw blood soaking through the short sleeve of Zohra's summer uniform. It seemed more than a simple scratch to him, but Zohra still clung to the steering wheel with both hands, while his right foot held down the accelerator pedal.

"Nothing, sir, I promise!" he repeated.

At a loss for words of comfort, Naseer barked, "Well, hold us steady, then! I'll pay them back in kind!"

He raised the AKMS to his shoulder once again, finding his mark, letting his index finger rest against the curved trigger. At the last instant, Naseer hesitated, more than half expecting another jolt to pitch him left or right, forward or back.

When nothing happened, he fired hastily, jerking the trigger, rather than applying steady pressure as he'd been instructed as a young recruit. The AKMS rattled in his ear and spewed out shiny brass, but Naseer would have been surprised if he had hit anything.

Another curse, before he braced himself, aiming. Naseer saw his opponent's lean face over open sights, already aiming back at him with what appeared to be—

The world exploded suddenly, without a hint of warning, and Tarik Naseer spun into crimson darkness.

THE GP-25 GRENADE launcher was nicknamed Kostyor— "bonfire," in Russian. The under-the-barrel model attached to Bolan's AKMS rifle measured about 12.5 inches long and weighed 3.3 pounds with an empty chamber. Breech-loading of a caseless 40 mm VOG-25 fragmentation grenade added half a pound to the deadly package, including 48 grams of high explosives.

Other grenades were readily available for the GP-25, including a bouncing frag round designated as the VOG-25P, Gvozd rounds filled with CS gas, baton rounds, and GRD smoke grenades designed for use at 50, 100 and 200 meters. Since Bolan's target was a moving vehicle, he chose the basic impact round for maximum effect.

Bolan slipped his left thumb through a hole provided in the launcher's stubby pistol grip, steadied his aim as best he could and sent the HE round downrange as one of his pursuers was about to try another autoburst. The Executioner's grenade got there first, slamming into the Jeep's grille and detonating on impact.

The result exceeded Bolan's hopes.

He'd thought that it would trash the Jeep's engine, shake up the driver and his passenger, granting Hussein Gorshani time to leave them in the dust before the APC caught up. Instead, the Jeep itself seemed to explode, hood airborne on a ball of fire, before it flipped through a clumsy forward somersault.

"Allah be praised!" Gorshani cried, catching the action in his rearview mirror.

Bolan didn't care who got the credit, and he knew that they weren't out of danger yet.

"There's still the APC," he said. "I won't crack that with 40 mm frag grenades."

"I can outrun them," Gorshani said.

"Now's the time to do it, then," Bolan answered.

In response, the SUV seemed to discover extra power somewhere underneath its hood. The truck surged forward, despite the rough ground underneath its tires. Thin carpet on the rear deck failed to cushion Bolan's spine and buttocks against heavy pounding.

He was lucky to have hit the Jeep at all, much less to stop it cold the way he had. Now Bolan saw the APC pull up beside the Jeep's wreckage and brake.

"They're stopping," he informed Gorshani. "Now's the time to give it everything you've got."

"I shall!" the Pakistani said, but their speed did not increase—it seemed the SUV had no more left to give. But still, every moment that the APC stayed where it was lengthened their lead.

"They've got someone up and moving," Bolan said. "He's in the vehicle. They're coming!"

Bolan did the math in his head. Say the SUV was traveling at sixty miles per hour, pulling steadily away. The APC would soon accelerate to its top speed of fifty miles per hour. It could never catch Gorshani's ride at that speed, all things being equal.

But they *weren't* equal.

The APC was built for travel over this type of terrain. Gorshani's SUV, despite its four-wheel-drive capacity, could not compete with the military vehicle in the long run.

And there was still the APC's machine gunner to reckon with. His PKM machine gun had a muzzle velocity of 2,500 feet per second, with a maximum range of 1,000 meters. It could rip through a belt of 650 rounds in 60 seconds and land a fair number of bullets on target at 200 meters.

The bottom line: if something happened to the SUV, or if the gunner in the APC got lucky, they were dead.

It would require a daring move to prevent either one of those events, and while that kind of play was Bolan's stock-in-trade, he didn't know whether Gorshani had the nerve to pull it off.

Fleeing from adversaries in a high-speed chase was one thing. Meeting them head-on was something else completely.

"They're gaining on us," Bolan said.

Gorshani muttered something Bolan took to be a curse, then said, "It won't go any faster."

"I don't want you to," Bolan replied.

"What, then?" Gorshani's eyes, reflected in the rearview mirror, held a hint of desperation.

"Slow down," Bolan told him. "Let them catch us."

THE EXECUTIONER knew he couldn't penetrate the BTR-70's armor with anything in his mobile arsenal. His 40 mm frag grenades would merely glance off the APC's nose to explode in midair—no threat to the soldiers inside. But he still had one chance.

"Slow down?" Gorshani questioned, from the driver's seat.

"And stop, when I give you the word," Bolan said.

The mirror-eyes met his again, for a heartbeat, then shifted away.

"As you wish."

Bolan fed the GP-25 another fragmentation round, as Gorshani raised his foot from the accelerator, letting the SUV decelerate without using the brakes. Behind them, the APC was gaining steadily, a juggernaut that seemed intent on running them down.

But that wasn't how it was done. Bolan knew his adversaries wouldn't ram Gorshani's vehicle if they had any other choice.

And they also had a machine gunner, who likely craved an opportunity to see some action.

A gunner who could only fire his weapon if he first revealed himself.

Bolan was ready when the hatch opened, a soldier's head and shoulders rising into view behind the pintle-mounted PKM. The Executioner fired his 40 mm round, then shouted at Gorshani, "Stop! Stop *now!*"

The SUV slid to a halt and Bolan rolled over the tailgate, conscious of the HE detonation eighty yards in front of him. He didn't see the nearly headless soldier topple backward, dropping through the hatch and almost landing in the driver's lap. Success was measured by the fact that no one riddled him with bullets as he charged the APC.

That vehicle slowed for a moment, lurching. It was just enough of a delay for Bolan to sprint across the intervening distance and launch into a leap from ten feet out.

The APC was nine feet tall, from ground level to the apex of its turret, but the fenders were about waist-high. Bolan's leap put him there, but it was not his final destination. Taking full advantage of the shock his 40 mm round had caused, he scrambled upward, toward the open hatch.

And as he reached it, Bolan held an RGD-5 frag grenade in his left hand. He yanked its safety pin at the last instant, dropped the bomb through the open hatch, then crouched and found a handhold on the turret's flank.

The grenade had a four-second fuse, granting zero time for anyone inside the APC to pick it up and throw it back. The blast reminded Bolan of a cherry bomb inside an oil drum, multiplied to the tenth power. Smoke and screams poured from the open hatch, as the APC lurched to a halt.

Bolan waited, knowing that one of two things had to happen next. The soldiers who could move would spill out through the APC's exit doors, or someone would lurch forward to take over from the mangled driver.

In the latter event, he would feed them another grenade. If they bailed—

Bolan heard the rear doors open, soldiers cursing as they scrambled from the smoky, blood-spattered interior. Their boots crunched on sand, losing traction as the men stumbled out.

The BTR-70 had room inside it for a three-man crew, plus seven passengers. Bolan had killed one of the crew with his first shot, and guessed the other two were dead or dying from the RGD-5's blast. How many others had been hit by shrapnel from the frag grenade? And how many of *those* were still fit to fight?

He strode across the flat top of the APC and caught the soldiers as they tried to organize—four men armed with Kalashnikovs, two of them with bloodstains showing on their desert-camo uniforms.

Their blood, or someone else's?

Bolan didn't care.

His AKMS raked the four men from left to right, then back again, making them dance as bullets ripped through flesh and fabric, dropping them before they could return fire. Bolan waited for another moment, covering the exit hatch. When no one else emerged, he readied himself for the nine-foot drop, prepared to check out the interior. Just as he flexed his knees to jump, he heard a scraping sound behind him.

One of the shell-shocked soldiers had been strong and smart enough to flank him. Now, unless Bolan could spin and drop at the same time, fire from the hip and nail the man who meant to kill him—

Halfway through his turn, Bolan flinched at the report of a Kalashnikov on autofire. Already braced to take the bullets that he knew were coming, the big American blinked, surprised to see his would-be slayer sprawled across the APC's gun turret, facedown in a spreading pool of blood.

"He's dead, I think," Gorshani called up to him from the ground.

"I'd say you're right," Bolan replied. "Now, let's get out of here."

4

Mount Khakwani, North-West Frontier Province

The messenger's name was Harata Bhutani. At thirty-four, he was the youngest man permitted access to the leaders of al Qaeda in hiding. All of the command staff's other aides were ten or twelve years older—and, of course, they all were men.

Akram Ben Abd al-Bari would not trust a woman—even his own mother, were she living—with the knowledge of his whereabouts, much less his current plans. To him and those around him, granting any power to a woman reeked of sacrilege.

Bhutani drove his battered motorcycle up a narrow, winding mountain road that was, at least in theory, wide enough for a small sedan. He didn't like to think about what might occur if two cars traveling in opposite directions met each other on the road. There was no room to pass, much less to turn around, and driving in reverse, he thought, would have been tantamount to suicide.

It's not my problem, he consoled himself. Bhutani did not own a car and never would. He had a driver's license, chiefly for delivery of martyrs to the towns where they would detonate the vests of high explosives hidden underneath their robes. On such occasions the car was always provided by his masters, and then discarded after it had served its purpose.

The small bike that he rode now, with its imported Chinese engine, cost 37,000 rupees in a showroom—about 575 U.S.

dollars. Bhutani had only paid roughly half of that, considering its age, but it had served him well.

One more trip to the mountains, basking in the modest glory of al Qaeda's leadership. Despite years of faithful service, the trust with which they honored him was more than Bhutani had any right to expect.

He knew when to expect the guards, black-turbaned and wearing peasant garb, with their Kalashnikov rifles and mismatched pistols tucked into their belts. They recognized him, but demanded that he speak the password, as if none of them had ever met before.

Security was everything, and rightly so.

When they were satisfied, the riflemen allowed Bhutani to proceed. The last two hundred yards comprised the steepest bit of highway on the mountain, rising toward a crest above the hidden caves—Bhutani's destination. Only those with business in the caves ever lived to reach them.

More guards waited for him at a turnout, where he killed the motorcycle's engine and dismounted, willingly surrendering the grenade, pistol and dagger that he carried every waking moment of his life. Bhutani then submitted to a search that would have been humiliating under any other circumstances.

Finally, the last phalanx of killers stood aside. One of them turned and led him back along a worn stony path, even though Bhutani could have navigated the trail in his sleep, blindfolded.

His escort left him at the cave's mouth, frowned in parting, and was gone. Bhutani stepped into the mountain's maw alone.

"WHAT WORD?" Akram Ben Abd al-Bari asked the messenger. Ra'id Ibn Rashad sat to his right, while two gunmen with checkered scarves obscuring the faces underneath their turbans stood on guard to either side.

"Masters," Bhutani said, "the struggle progresses. Martyrs have completed their angelic sacrifice in Kabul, Kandahar, Qunduz and Ghazni. At the present time, we estimate one hundred dead, four times that number wounded. In Kabul, the count includes seven Crusaders."

"Excellent," al-Bari said.

He knew the body count might be exaggerated slightly, for his own benefit, but no one in the ranks would risk an outright fabrication. The resultant penalties would be severe, protracted and irreparable.

"What of Iraq?" Rashad inquired.

"The conflict that Crusaders choose to call an *insurrection* serves us well," Bhutani said. "Each day, we welcome new recruits. The pool of volunteers for martyrdom is constantly replenished, spurred on by the actions of the invaders and their lackeys in Baghdad. Selective executions of the Shiite leadership continue. One sad note…"

Bhutani hesitated, lowering his eyes.

"Proceed," al-Bari said.

"Abdul Aliyy Ibn Nidal is dead, slain by the agents of Mossad, we think, in Amsterdam. A car bomb."

Well, al-Bari thought, live by the sword…

"He waits for us in Paradise," Rashad intoned.

Al-Bari nodded, but his thoughts were not with Nidal's mangled body, lying on a bloodstained street in Holland. Rather, he was thinking once again about the facts of life that forced him to receive such news by word of mouth, sometimes delayed for days. A television or a shortwave radio would have made life much simpler. But with all the tracking satellites circling the planet, beaming signals earthward to al-Bari's enemies, modern communications might have spelled the end of life for him.

His guards used simple two-way radios—handheld devices sold at any electronics shop, range limited to half a mile or less. Al-Bari had convinced himself that they could not be monitored by enemies, as long as their transmissions were irregular and brief.

But for the rest, for passing orders down the ranks and waiting to discover whether victory was his, or if valued comrades had been slaughtered by their foes, al-Bari now relied upon the oldest method of communication known to man.

"What of the project in Islamabad?" he asked Bhutani.

"Ready to proceed on your command, master."

"Let it proceed."

Bhutani bowed his head in mute acknowledgment.

"On your way out," al-Bari ordered, "send in Arzou Majabein."

THE BATTLEFIELD was far behind them. Far enough, at least, for Bolan to relax a bit and to begin debriefing his contact. Hussein Gorshani, for his part, still seemed nervous, eyes flicking back and forth between his rearview mirror and the road ahead.

"Nobody's chasing us," Bolan advised him.

"No. Not yet," the driver said.

"You think they radioed ahead?"

"Why not? It's possible."

"We should have seen the reinforcements rolling in by now," Bolan replied. "We're clear. For the moment."

"I just didn't expect…I mean, so soon."

"Neither did I," Bolan admitted.

Had it been bad luck, or something far more sinister.

"You weren't followed?" he asked Gorshani for the second time since their narrow escape.

"I swear it! I took every possible precaution."

"And you didn't let it slip to anyone, where you were going?"

"I am not a fool," Gorshani said, sounding offended now.

"Accidents happen."

"Not if one is cautious."

"Fair enough. Call it a random patrol. Wrong time, wrong place."

"I hope so," Gorshani said, sounding less convinced by his own argument than he had previously.

"It's the only way to play it," Bolan said, closing the subject. "Now, tell me more about al-Bari's hideout."

"I received the information from my contact in Islamabad," Gorshani said. "He is, how do you say, my *handler* in such things."

"That's how you say it," Bolan granted.

"Such a term could be interpreted as an insult, I think, but never mind. I understand it."

"So?"

"It was a strange thing, yes? I am supposed to give him information, not receive it. Yet, he visits me the other day and says that a man is coming who will strike against al Qaeda. He tells me I must guide this man to a certain place, and then he gives me the approximate location."

"When you say 'approximate'..."

"He named a mountain in the Safed Koh range, near the border with Afghanistan. It's also known in Pashto as the Morga Range—white mountains."

"And the mountain is...?"

"Mount Khakwani, south of Mount Sikaram, but not so tall. Perhaps two thousand meters."

"Nobody mentioned climbing gear," Bolan observed.

"We can obtain what you would call the basics on our way. The climb should not be arduous, although we cannot use the road."

Bolan wondered if Brognola had known that, or if the fact had been withheld from him by someone higher up the bureaucratic ladder. Either way, it further complicated Bolan's task, which had been perilous enough without a fling at mountaineering.

"And once we've climbed the mountain, then what?" Bolan asked.

"I'm told the road on Mount Khakwani passes caves, where those you seek are now concealed. They are located near the summit. And knowing that, it would seem to me that once we have reached the proper altitude, we could simply follow footpaths on the mountainside—and there they are!"

Simply, Bolan thought, nearly smiling at the driver's choice of adjectives.

"Should be a piece of cake, then, right?" he said.

"A piece of cake?"

"Forget it. How far is it to al-Bari's mountain?"

"Across the Kunar River, then another sixty-five kilometers. But first, we stop at Sanjrani. It is a village where I have a friendly source for climbing gear."

"Are the police friendly?" Bolan inquired.

"There are no resident police in Sanjrani. As for army patrols or Frontier Corps, we take our chances, yes? Hoping to be in the right place, at the right time."

"You do the talking," Bolan said. "But if it starts to fall apart, stand clear."

"The people of Sanjrani will not harm us. I am sure of them," Gorshani said, and then amended, "*Most* of them."

"Then all we have to do," Bolan replied, "is watch out for the rest."

ARZOU MAJABEIN followed the narrow corridor of stone, with daylight fading at his back, until he reached a heavy curtain hung across the rough-hewn entrance to Akram Ben Abd al-Bari's receiving chamber. Passing two armed guards, he slipped past the curtain and advanced to kneel before a low stone platform in the middle of the room.

Seated before him on a humble pad of blankets were the men he served. Akram Ben Abd al-Bari sat to Majabein's right, and Ra'id Ibn Rashad to his left. Their bodyguards, stationed on either side of the two seated men, might have been carved from wax for all the animation they displayed.

Majabein bowed, his forehead almost touching the stone floor, and asked, "How may I serve you, masters?"

"You will take a message to our friend in Rawalpindi," Rashad said.

"Yes, sir."

There was no need to ask which friend. Rawalpindi, south-west of Islamabad on the Punjab Plateau, hosted headquarters for the Pakistan armed forces. Only one man of importance there was allied with al Qaeda. But even here, in the one place on Earth where they should feel secure, al-Bari and Rashad refused to speak his name aloud.

"Tell him," al-Bari said, "that we have always appreciated his aid, but we observe the tide of government accommodation for the Great Satan. Islamabad accepts money and guns from Washington, then uses them to harass freedom fighters. We believed removal of the woman would convey our disapproval, but the message was ignored."

Again, there was no need to ask which woman al-Bari referred to.

"We are informed," al-Bari said, "that the Crusaders are reopening their church and school within Islamabad. We view this plan with disfavor and believe that it should not proceed."

That statement came as no surprise. An attack on Islamabad's historic Christian church in March 2002 had killed five persons and wounded forty-six. Since the Crusaders failed to get the message, six more died in an August raid against the nearby Christian school.

It would seem, the infidels had forgotten that lesson.

"Tell our friend," al-Bari said, "that an example must be made. A martyr's sacrifice may serve, where other methods have failed."

Majabein suppressed a frown. He could not predict how their friend at military headquarters would react to news of an impending bomb attack in the nation's capital. If the reaction was adverse, it would be Majabein himself who felt the first sting of the lash, but he could not refuse the call.

He lived to serve.

Rashad spoke next. "Inform our friend," he said, "that we desire no martyrs among the faithful other than our chosen one. Any Sunni carpenters or other workmen hired by the

Crusaders should be sick at home tomorrow. Tell them to repent for serving Allah's enemies, and caution them that any further sin against our holy cause will not merit forgiveness."

"As you say, masters, so let it be."

"We have considered that our friend may show some reticence," al-Bari said. "If that should prove to be the case, remind him that he owes a debt of honor to al Qaeda. We have no desire for him to be embarrassed…or removed."

"I understand," Majabein said.

"You are dismissed," al-Bari said. "May Allah speed you on your way."

"My thanks to you, masters."

After bowing once more, Majabein rose and backed away from the chamber, turning only when he felt the heavy curtain brush against his backside. From that point on, he moved briskly along the tunnel corridor to daylight, passing guards who would forget his face as soon as he was out of sight.

He had important work to do.

And like the targets in Islamabad who were condemned, Majabein was running out of time.

Army Headquarters, Rawalpindi

BRIGADIER BAHAAR Jadoon cradled the telephone receiver with exaggerated care and turned to face Colonel Salim Laghari. "It's confirmed," he said. "All twelve are dead."

Jadoon supposed the colonel's scowl was less for twelve dead soldiers than for some concern of potential damage to his reputation and career.

"Sir, we must strike without delay," Laghari said.

"At whom, Colonel?" Jadoon inquired.

The question stumped his junior officer for several heartbeats, then Laghari said, "It is obvious that rebels are responsible."

"Indeed? Which ones?"

Another hesitation on the colonel's part.

Within the North-West Frontier Province, there were several "militia" groups at war with one another. Sunnis killing Shiites and vice versa. Smugglers running weapons, drugs and other contraband across the border, to and from Afghanistan. Any faction, if taken by surprise or threatened, might fire on a government patrol.

But to annihilate a dozen soldiers and destroy an armored vehicle, now, that took skill.

Laghari took the safe road, saying, "Sir, we should respond with force throughout the area. Arrest and punish weapons dealers. Institute a sweep to drive guerrillas from the province."

And send them where? Jadoon was on the verge of asking, but he held his tongue. Colonel Laghari's anger and frustration were predictable. Jadoon felt much the same himself, but there were still certain realities to be observed.

Sweeping guerrillas from the North-West Frontier Province had been tried before, on numerous occasions, and the effort had always failed. In that event, the person subject to demotion, transfer and a slow death for his once promising career would be the officer who had given the order to proceed.

And Jadoon did not intend to be that man.

He planned to be a general someday, but that meant climbing three more ranks, obtaining three more stars to decorate his uniform, instead of being slapped down to the grade of colonel—or, worse, yet, lieutenant colonel. Jadoon would be taking orders from Laghari, then, and that would be unbearable.

"Colonel," Jadoon replied, "I think you're onto something. Any move we make, of course, must first be based on sound intelligence. Agreed?"

"Yes, sir!"

"With that in mind, I'm sending you to take charge of the

inquiry and follow every lead available. You will report to me twice daily, at a minimum, by radio or telephone."

Colonel Laghari wore a vague expression of surprise. "Sir, when you say investigate—"

"I mean precisely that. Examine the location of the ambush, whatever evidence may be available, then seek out any witnesses from the surrounding countryside. Interrogate known malcontents and arms dealers. You understand? Investigate."

"Yes, sir. But—"

"It may take some time, I realize. Don't worry about that. Lieutenant Colonel Davi will assume your duties, in your absence. He's a capable young officer, don't you agree?"

"Yes, sir, apparently. But I wonder if—"

"You'll need to seek assistance from Frontier Corps, of course. And don't forget the Federal Investigation Agency. This is primarily a military matter, naturally, but any massacre of active-duty troops also raises the broader question of security across the board."

"Sir, if I may—"

"You'll need to leave at once, Colonel. No time for tying up loose ends around the office, I'm afraid. Leave everything to me…and to Lieutenant Colonel Davi. He can use your office while you're gone, eh? Good. Dismissed!"

Colonel Laghari stiffened to attention, snapped off a salute, then turned and marched out of the office, pausing only long enough to shut the door. Jadoon circled his desk, sat down and smiled.

He had not solved the problem of the murdered soldiers, but he *had* removed a sharp stone from his shoe, however temporarily. Colonel Laghari was ambitious, even avaricious. And, worse yet, Jadoon had reason to believe he was a spy for someone higher up who sought to meddle with the brigadier's career. Jadoon could not yet take action against the man behind Laghari, but he was well accustomed to the military regimen of hurry up and wait.

If he could place Laghari in an awkward situation, even one where danger was involved, so much the better. Of course, if Laghari's investigation of the ambush failed to bring results—or if he made things worse somehow, by agitating groups with no connection to the incident—it would be the colonel's career that suffered, not his.

And if Laghari somehow managed to discover those responsible for the attack, Bahaar Jadoon would claim the credit, for assigning Laghari to investigate.

It was what the Americans might call a win-win situation for the brigadier.

And now, if only he could really find out why twelve of his men had died…

HUSSEIN GORSHANI took his time driving along the poorly maintained two-lane blacktop that passed for a highway in the Pakistani hinterlands. Bolan slumped in the shotgun seat, trying to minimize his height compared to the driver's, eyes alternately scanning the road ahead and the reflected image in his side mirror.

So far, no one was chasing them, and they had seen no reinforcements rushing toward the battle site from the direction they were heading. The Executioner ticked off details in his mind that he had memorized about the opposition they might face, before they reached the Safed Koh range and began to scale Mount Khakwani.

In addition to its massive standing army, Pakistan maintained five separate paramilitary forces, tasked to cover different geographical areas and aspects of national defense. Units of the 185,000-member Pakistan National Guard were scattered nationwide, officially divided into the Janbaz and Mujahid Forces, designed to supplement regular army units at need. The Pakistan Rangers, with 30,000 men under arms, were divided between Lahore and Karachi, and should not concern him. Likewise, the Mehran Force—some 25,000 men, restricted to the Sindh Province—would not be involved in Bolan's mission. And he flatly dismissed the Maritime Security Agency, a coast guard operation with 2,500 sworn personnel.

Only the Frontier Corps, acting in collaboration with the regular army, threatened to frustrate Bolan's operation. It claimed 60,000 men, roughly divided between the North-West Frontier Province and neighboring Baluchistan, with command-rank officers reporting both to army headquarters and to the Ministry of States and Frontier Regions. Frontier Corps units could be "regularized" at need, in the event of war or other national emergencies, but they were fully capable of hunting on their own.

The men Bolan and Gorshani had eliminated earlier were army regulars. Their uniforms, insignia and markings on their vehicles told Bolan that. With that in mind, he knew the army would be hunting them before long—if they weren't, already—and headquarters would be pulling out all stops to do the job.

It wouldn't take them long to find Bolan's abandoned parachute, but that would lead them nowhere. Prior to packing, it was stripped of any labels or identifying marks that might have helped his adversaries trace it to a manufacturer or seller. He supposed a lab could break down the fabric and trace it that way, taking days or weeks, but by then the Executioner's mission would be finished.

One way or the other.

Even if Bolan failed, his corpse and gear would tell the Pakistanis nothing they could use.

But Bolan didn't plan to fail.

He didn't plan to die in Pakistan, chasing a pair of men who had evaded thousands for the past nine years.

At home, he knew that questions had been raised concerning laggardly pursuit of those responsible for 9/11. Many thought that in this day of smart bombs and satellite photos that could read a newspaper headline or license plate number from outer space, locating fugitives had become a simple matter of pressing a button and watching an address appear.

But hunting a determined fugitive who had resources of his own, and who could operate without reliance on "the grid," was not much different in the twenty-first-century Middle East than it had been in the nineteenth-century Old West. Manhunters on the ground were still required to follow tracks, grill witnesses and sort through leads that might have been established to mislead them in the first place.

And, along the way, they would sometimes find themselves engaged in battles to survive.

It was a down-and-dirty job, but someone had to do it.

And this day, it was Bolan's turn.

No sweat.

It was the kind of job he'd done before, and doubtless would again—assuming he survived this time around.

And at the bottom line, survival was his business.

He had that much in common with Akram Ben Abd al-Bari and Ra'id Ibn Rashad—and the resemblance didn't end there.

In their own ways, all of them were executioners.

"Ten miles to Sanjrani," Gorshani said.

Bolan nodded and closed his eyes.

5

Arzou Majabein never considered walking into army head-quarters an option, although the man he was supposed to meet worked from an office there. His face adorned a Wanted poster in that building, and while the average soldier or policeman on the street made no attempt to locate him on any given day, if he strolled past them in the corridors of their own building, they would be forced to arrest him.

Even in a nation such as Pakistan, which hovered on the brink of lawlessness, certain appearances had to be preserved.

Majabein *had* telephoned his contact at the office, using the name they had agreed upon—Rahim Mengal—to leave a message. When the coded language had been stripped away, it called for Brigadier Bahaar Jadoon to meet him in the city's central marketplace at six o'clock, for the delivery of an important message that could not be trusted to the telephone.

Majabein did not tell Jadoon to wear civilian clothes. Such advice was unnecessary with a man of Jadoon's advanced position and presumed intelligence.

Of course, if he had truly been intelligent, Jadoon would not have owed his rank and ongoing existence to al Qaeda, but such was life.

Majabein moved slowly through the market stalls, pretending to browse while he worked his way toward the selected rendezvous point. Anything that a person might need was on sale at the market—except, in this case, firearms. It would have embarrassed the army to have guns on show within blocks of its primary headquarters.

Rawalpindi's gun mart was a mile away, "concealed" within an open warehouse that did business around the clock.

Which did not mean there were no guns in Rawalpindi's marketplace. Majabein himself carried a Chinese Type 59 semiautomatic pistol, copied from the classic Russian Makarov in 9 mm. Beneath his loose shirt, he also concealed a hand grenade clipped to his belt.

Just in case.

Jadoon was waiting at the stall where knives were sold and sharpened when Majabein arrived. They went through the pantomime of a chance encounter, each supposing that the other had to have bodyguards—although, in fact, both men had come alone.

Majabein spurned escorts because they slowed him down.

Jadoon worried that anyone who shared his secret would betray him.

After they had spent a moment admiring the knife maker's work, the two men moved off through the crowd, appearing for all the world to be casual friends. If anyone had trailed them, close enough to overhear their conversation, the eavesdropper would have been surprised.

"I bring a warning," Majabein announced, once they were moving.

"From…?"

"Our masters."

"Ah."

"The Christians in Islamabad have grown too arrogant. They must be taught their proper place."

"And what do you propose."

"Not I," Majabein said.

"Of course. Your masters, then?"

"And yours, lest you forget."

Was that a flare of hatred in Jadoon's dark eyes? If so, it

did not worry Majabein. He knew who held the reins in this relationship.

"What sort of lesson?" Jadoon asked.

"Tomorrow, at midday, a martyr is prepared to sacrifice himself for Allah where the infidels gather to pray. You know the place?"

"Of course," Jadoon replied.

And well he should, since it had been the site of the 2002 attacks.

"I tell you this," Majabein said, "because our masters felt that you might wish to clear the area of the faithful prior to the event."

Jadoon drew back his head, peering at Majabein along the steep slope of his nose. "And how would you suggest I accomplish that, without alerting others?" he inquired.

"It should be relatively simple," Majabein opined. "Perhaps a bit of street construction in the neighborhood would serve the purpose. Have a couple of your soldiers or policemen redirect shoppers to other stores until the time has passed."

"And the Christians?"

"Of course, they must be granted access to their church," Majabein said. "Admit them to the street, by all means. Otherwise, they might complain."

"You have suggested barring Muslims from the street. How would your martyr, then, be able to achieve his goal?"

"Even the best guards make mistakes, sometimes."

"How would they know which Muslim *not* to notice?"

"They will know him by his youth, his walk, his smile."

Jadoon was frowning underneath his thick mustache. "The timing of this incident," he said, "is not…convenient."

"For whom?" Majabein asked sharply.

"For anyone. Our government is under scrutiny by the Americans, concerning military aid agreements authorized by the prime minister. They still complain that we—meaning the state—grant sanctuary to known terrorists. If this event proceeds, it gives them one more thing to criticize and point to as evidence."

Majabein's shrug betrayed no interest in Jadoon's problems. "A martyr dies," he said. "The case is solved."

"Crusaders want the men behind the martyr. You know that, as well as I do."

"Then, they must be disappointed, eh?"

"I'm not sure how much longer I can cover for the men you serve," Jadoon replied. "If I am ordered to proceed, I can't defy field marshals, much less the prime minister himself."

"You owe the men *we* serve two lives," Majabein said. "Have you forgotten that?"

"I have forgotten nothing."

Pressing on as if Jadoon had not replied, Majabein said, "First, there was the woman. Just a worthless prostitute, I realize, but still… If we had not concealed her death, think of the scandal and its cost. You would have lost your precious job, your family—and then, most likely, your head. Do you remember?"

"Yes," Jadoon hissed.

"And the officer who hated you? Who had pledged himself to sidetrack your promotion to lieutenant colonel and to any rank beyond it? Did the men *we* serve not make him disappear, as if by magic?"

"So they did." Jadoon sounded defeated now.

"It's good to be reminded of such things from time to time," Majabein said. "I trust you have no problem with the timing of our martyr's sacrifice, my friend?"

"No problem," Jadoon said.

"In that case, rest assured that *we* have no problem with *you.*"

Sanjrani Village, North-West Frontier Province

THERE WAS NO SUCH thing as absolute security. In fact, Bolan had learned from personal experience that governments that focused single-mindedly on any given aspect of security—be it eradication of dissent, suppression of illegal immigration, or a "war" on contraband of any kind—not only failed, but actually drove lawbreakers to invent new means of violating rules and regulations.

And so it was in Pakistan, created as a separate state after bloody riots between Muslims and Hindus in India. But the conflict was never truly settled. Pakistan and India had battled over the disputed Kashmir territory since 1947. There have been four full-scale wars and various guerrilla actions, including most recently a firebombing of the Samjhauta Express between Delhi and Lahore that killed sixty-eight passengers in February 2007.

The relative quiet since then proved nothing—except that the action had shifted, at least in part, to Pakistan's western border. There, abutting Afghanistan, al Qaeda and the Taliban were still fighting to regain their old ground and expel the Coalition troops who had broken their grip on Afghanistan in 2001.

In such an atmosphere, where illegal gun sales flourished, many villages had become armed camps in order to survive. Sanjrani was a case in point, as Gorshani explained to Bolan.

"The people there are not our enemies," he said. "They hate al Qaeda. But, of course, they don't know you."

"Do they know you?" Bolan inquired.

"My mother came from Sanjrani. I still have family there."

"And they don't mind you dropping by with strangers packing guns?"

"They will not question it," Gorshani said.

Was there a hint of doubt around the driver's eyes? Bolan preferred not to consider it, since he was counting on Sanjrani's villagers to furnish the supplies they'd need for climbing the mountain.

"No problem, sir. I'm sure of it," Gorshani said.

But did he speak for Bolan's benefit or to just convince himself?

The last two miles of highway leading to Sanjrani ran through forest that pressed close on either side. As afternoon faded to evening, shadows lurked among the trees and seemed to race along beside Gorshani's SUV, pacing the vehicle. The optical illusion prompted Bolan to recall old paintings in which wolves pursued the passengers of horse-drawn sleighs and carriages.

"Would there be any wolves around this area?" Bolan asked.

"Wolves? Perhaps," Gorshani said. "They're found more often in Baluchistan, but sometimes here. Jackals are much more common, I must say."

Same thing in my world, Bolan thought, but kept it to himself.

A moment later, Bolan saw the village up ahead. It was a smudge on the horizon at first, but rapidly grew until his eyes could pick out various specific buildings. People moved among the structures, disappearing as the SUV drew closer.

"Anybody know that we were coming?" Bolan asked.

"They know," Gorshani said. "But until they have seen me, they don't know who is approaching."

Right. Of course.

"I hope they aren't a bunch of nervous types," Bolan said.

"They won't shoot without good reason," his companion said. "I promise you."

"Well, let's not give them any reason, then," the Executioner replied.

COLONEL SALIM Laghari was an officer who followed orders, even when he did not understand them fully—or when he did not believe that they made sense.

For example, it made no sense, in his mind, that he should leave Rawalpindi to conduct a personal investigation of the ambush that had killed twelve soldiers in the North-West Frontier Province. But because he had been sent here by Brigadier Jadoon, Laghari meant to do the best job possible.

In fact, he meant to find the criminals responsible for the attack and bring them in for trial as terrorists.

Assuming that any survived the manhunt.

Colonel Laghari had recognized Jadoon's suspicion of him from the moment he was transferred to the brigadier's command. In Laghari's experience, that kind of instant, unprovoked reaction said something about a person's character.

Jadoon distrusted Laghari because he—Jadoon—had something to fear. There had to be something in his past, or in his present, that would damage him if it should be revealed. Colonel Laghari probably would not have tried to find out what that was, if Brigadier Jadoon had simply treated him as one more officer with ordinary duties to perform.

But now…

Suspect a spy, he thought, and sometimes you create a spy.

Laghari had not found Jadoon's dark secret yet, but he was looking. Slowly, cautiously, making no moves that would expose himself to risk, he burrowed from within, keeping his eyes and ears open. Someday, somehow, he would discover what the brigadier was frightened of coming to light.

And when that day came, it would be his turn to give orders.

In the meantime, though, Laghari went where he was told to go and did what he was told to do. In this case—tracking down the murderers of soldiers in the field—his orders coincided with his sense of duty.

He had brought four men along with him, in one of the army's Bell 407 light transport helicopters. Upon arrival in Peshawar, the provincial capital, Laghari had presented his orders from Brigadier Jadoon and commandeered another sixteen men, along with two M113 armored personnel carriers. He did not requisition a Jeep, in light of what had befallen the last one, preferring instead to ride with his men under armor.

The M113s were tracked vehicles weighing twelve tons each and mounting Browning M2 .50-caliber machine guns on their turrets. The armor was 1.5-inches thick, versus .35 inches on the BTR-70 APC, while the M113 had a top speed of about 66 mph, against the BTR's 50 mph. Both vehicles had two-man crews, with extra room for eleven passengers.

Colonel Laghari believed he was prepared for anything. Except failure.

Rolling along the potholed rural highway, buttoned up inside the APC, Laghari focused on the problem of Bahaar Jadoon in order to distract himself from his discomfort. The vehicles were air-conditioned, but the stream of tepid air did little to prevent Laghari and the other weapons-laden passengers from sweating. It had smelled like an unsanitary locker room when he had crawled through the hatch to take his hard, uncomfortable seat, and nothing had improved as the small convoy drove northward underneath a broiling sun.

After considering the risks involved, Laghari had armed himself with a standard-issue pistol and a Heckler & Koch MP-5 submachine gun. He had qualified with both weapons in basic training, but advancement through the peacetime ranks had thus far spared Laghari from the need to fire at living targets. He was not concerned about his capability, however.

If and when an adversary tried to kill him, Laghari was confident he'd have no problem defending himself.

A crewman's voice over the intercom informed Laghari that they had reached their destination. He let the other soldiers exit from the APC before him, then stepped out and saw the first of two wrecked military vehicles.

It seemed the Scorpion Jeep had taken some kind of direct hit to the grille from an explosive charge, and had then cartwheeled from the impact, spilling its passengers in the process. The bodies had been carted off to a morgue, where Laghari could view them later, if he chose to.

Beyond the Jeep, Laghari saw the burned-out BTR-70 where the rest of the soldiers had died. A grenade through the hatch, he was told, followed by automatic weapons fire when the survivors had scrambled from the APC. As for the means by which the enemy had approached the vehicle and managed to deposit his explosive charge inside, no one had yet suggested to Laghari how such a thing had been possible.

Despite the late afternoon's oppressive heat, Laghari felt a sudden chill. He recognized the fear for what it was, tried to suppress it immediately, and hoped he had at least succeeded in concealing it from his subordinates around him.

The people who had committed this act were long gone.

Laghari's mission was to find them and bring them to justice, one way or another. He had no training as a field investigator—a fact well-known to Brigadier Jadoon—but he was not entirely helpless.

When seeking answers, one asked questions.

And kept asking, more forcefully each time, until the proper answer was received.

Turning to a lieutenant on his left, Laghari asked, "Where is the nearest village to this place?"

Islamabad

BRIGADIER BAHAAR Jadoon surveyed the street where dozens, perhaps scores of people would be killed the following day, shortly after noon. Not simply killed, in fact, but torn apart by shrapnel, scorched by flames and buried in rubble.

He wondered whether some of those who passed him on the sidewalk now would be among the dead. Which of them would lose arms, legs, eyes to the bomb blast? Some young fool whom he had never met, whose name Jadoon might never learn, would walk along that very sidewalk with a beatific smile etched on his face and detonate the Semtex charges strapped under his clothes.

Yet plastique was not the end of it. Such bombs were built for maximum effect, complete with plastic bags of nails, screws, nuts and bolts, ball bearings—anything, in fact, that would extend their killing range. And if that was not bad enough, there might be other plastic bags stuffed full of rancid barnyard muck, to make wounds fester in the survivors.

The young man who had been chosen for that act of martyrdom would be drifting through the best day of his life. Jadoon knew how the martyrs were pampered during their final hours: bathed, perfumed, well-fed and dressed in freshly laundered clothing. Though security guards were trained to sniff them out, by the time you were able to smell their cologne—or the insecticide sprayed to kill flies on the bags filled with muck—it was likely too late.

The chosen martyr might spend the night praying, or possibly dreaming of Paradise, where a smiling Allah waited to receive him with thanks, conducting him to a verdant garden occupied by forty beautiful and oh-so-willing virgins. What was an instant of shattering pain, compared to an eternity of avid sex, with breaks for milk and honey?

"You see the problem?" Brigadier Jadoon asked his companion.

"The shops, of course, but we can deal with that," the second man replied. "Begin the quiet warnings about half-past ten. Work crews will be in place by then. Block off access around 11:45."

Jadoon's companion was Husna Chadhar, a captain with the army's Special Services Group, which operated in the shadow of Military Intelligence, but with a separate command structure and rule book. What the Americans called "dirty tricks" were for the SSG, and many of its operations were banned by Pakistani law.

As if that mattered.

Chadhar and Jadoon served the same masters—in more ways than one. While they were both army officers, they had not met until Majabein had introduced them, approximately two years earlier, during a secret meeting outside Rawalpindi. Since that time, they had collaborated on several delicate projects, acting on behalf of al Qaeda, but this would be their first excursion into mass murder.

"It's feasible, then?" Jadoon asked.

"As good as done," Chadhar replied.

"And the deniability?"

"My men don't carry tales. In any case, they'll simply think that we're engaged in a surveillance operation. When the bomb goes off, they will be suitably surprised."

"When you say we…?"

"I shall be here to supervise," Chadhar explained. "Something this delicate cannot be left to underlings. Imagine, if one of them tried to stop the boy."

Chadhar's bemused expression told Jadoon exactly what he thought of such benighted foolishness. It made him chuckle as he shook his head.

"And afterward?"

"Nothing," Chadhar replied. "We are construction workers, after all, not doctors. When the smoke clears, we'll be gone, no one the wiser. Any gear left at the scene by chance will prove untraceable."

Jadoon had wondered, many times, how Chadhar had come to serve al Qaeda. Had he been a convert to the cause? Or had he been ensnared by his own weakness, as had happened to Bahaar Jadoon? And did it even matter?

No.

The two of them were in this thing together, taking orders from a band of criminals, betraying every oath that they had sworn upon enlisting with the army.

Well, perhaps not every oath.

The Pakistani army's motto was Faith, Piety, to strive in the path of Allah.

Each member of al Qaeda, each fugitive combatant of the Taliban, believed that he was filled with faith and piety, devoted to pursuing Allah's path of righteous fury against infidels. Perhaps Chadhar felt just the same.

For Jadoon's part, he'd mouthed the motto on enlistment, without ever really giving it a moment's thought. Who really cared what soldiers believed in, as long as they followed orders, Jadoon surmised.

Gazing one last time along the street of busy shops, with the Christian church planted halfway down on his right, Jadoon closed his mind to the visions of carnage.

"Very well," he said. "Do it."

DUSK OVERTOOK Bolan and Gorshani as they entered the guide's ancestral village. Full darkness was still at least an hour off, but Bolan didn't fancy scaling mountains after nightfall, when they couldn't risk using a light and he was unfamiliar with the hostile ground.

"We'll need somewhere to stay the night," he said reluctantly.

"It is arranged," Gorshani said. "My mother's people."

"So, you think of everything?"

"It did not seem so, earlier," Gorshani said.

Thinking of how he'd dropped the shooter on the APC, Bolan replied, "You pulled your weight."

"I was...surprised," his driver said.

"There's nothing wrong with that," Bolan allowed, "as long as you survive it."

Watched by various Sanjrani residents, Gorshani turned his dusty SUV into a narrow side street, crept along its length, then turned again to park behind some kind of shop. Bolan assumed the news of their arrival would be spread by word-of-mouth, throughout the village and beyond. He only hoped Gorshani's faith in those who carried it was justified.

"Wait here, a moment," Gorshani said, then he climbed out of the car and walked around to knock on the small shop's back door. A moment passed before the door opened, revealing a gray-bearded man in a turban and peasant garb, wearing what looked like a permanent scowl.

Gorshani and the older man spoke briefly, then Gorshani beckoned Bolan from the SUV. Bolan made sure the key wasn't in the ignition, set the door locks as he exited and took his AKMS rifle with him as he ducked into the shop.

The bearded man did not seem worried or insulted by the sight of Bolan's weapons. In fact, after a quick preliminary once-over, he managed to ignore Bolan completely, conversing with Gorshani in rapid-fire Pashto as Gorshani read off his shopping list.

They started off with climbing ropes and static lines, carabiners and belay gloves for both men. Gorshani also chose a pack, canteens and sturdy hiking boots for himself. The shopkeeper directed them and put the items in a duffel bag. Gorshani translated for Bolan as they went along, and quoted him the final price.

It seemed exorbitant, but as Bolan recalled one Pakistan rupee was roughly equivalent to a cent and a half in U.S. currency. All things considered, the quote of forty thousand rupees wasn't bad.

Gorshani walked their gear back to the SUV with Bolan trailing him, checking both ways along the alley set behind Sanjrani's main street shops. The merchant who had served them didn't follow the men outside or even watch them leave, as far as Bolan could detect. His door was shut before they pulled away.

"Where next?" Bolan inquired.

"We're going to my uncle's home. I have arranged for us to spend the night there. It is safe."

Bolan saw no point in questioning whether Gorshani was sure of that fact. An ambush at his uncle's home spelled peril for the family, as well as for Bolan himself. He had no wish to jeopardize Sanjrani's citizens, but from a purely practical aspect, he knew they would be better off sleeping indoors, among the natives, than camping out in the open.

Angry, frightened soldiers would be searching for the slayers of their comrades by this time, inclined to shoot first and ask questions later—if at all.

One night was not so much to ask. Was it?

6

Qaimkhani, North-West Frontier Province

The village headman's name was Aarya Chaudhry. He was middle-aged and slender, bearded, dressed in a freshly ironed version of laborer's garb. He was six inches shorter than Colonel Salim Laghari, which immediately placed him at a disadvantage while they spoke.

Laghari liked that.

He was also pleased to be surrounded by a ring of soldiers, walling off himself and the village headman from the gathered peasants of Qaimkhani.

"You've seen no one from outside the village, since midday?" Laghari repeated his previous question, letting his tone and facial expression reveal his skepticism.

"No, sir," Chaudhry answered for the second time. "We have nothing for tourists here. The province has nothing for tourists. We are not on any main highway. Those travelers we see are only going back and forth from Khetran to Buzdaar."

"And you saw none of them? All day?"

Again he replied, "No, sir."

The headman's patience irked Laghari. Was he putting on a bland face for authority, while lying through his small gray teeth? Laghari couldn't tell, and he was nervous about using any stronger method of interrogation, when he had no evidence that those who'd ambushed the routine patrol had actually passed this way.

Routine patrol.

Laghari had confirmed that, to the best of his ability, although he knew it was entirely possible that he had been deceived, either by Brigadier Bahaar Jadoon or someone higher up. Though it struck him as unlikely that Jadoon would order an investigation, then proceed to guarantee its failure by withholding vital information.

Unlikely, but not unthinkable.

He tried another tack with Chaudhry. "When did you first learn of the attack on our patrol?"

"When you informed me of it, Colonel. In Qaimkhani we have only one good radio, and it is broken."

"No one brought the news by word-of-mouth?"

"Only yourself, sir," the man insisted.

Laghari was running out of questions. He had been staring at the headman, trying to come up with something else to ask him, when the high-pitched whining of a small engine intruded on his thoughts, completely jumbling them.

Laghari and his soldiers turned in the direction of the sound. They saw a young man—no, a teenager—approaching from the north along a narrow unpaved track. He rode a small motorcycle that had started life as a Stahlco 70 cc model, adding mismatched bits and pieces over time as its original components rusted out or suffered some irreparable harm.

The rider braked to a halt in front of Laghari's men, killed his engine and let the bike drop since it had no kickstand. He stepped closer to the troops, half bowed and told them, "Please, I need to see the officer in charge."

"Search him," Laghari ordered, watching as a pair of soldiers frisked the new arrival, then turned out his pockets, showing their pathetic contents to the colonel.

When he felt secure from a surprise attack, Laghari stepped forward, rapid-firing questions. "Who are you? Where have you come from? How did you find us? What brings you here?"

The young man waited for Laghari to run through his list, then started answering the inquiries in order.

"I am Mahmood Hasni," he said. "Sanjrani is my village. It lies…there." He turned and pointed vaguely, back along the route he had followed to reach Qaimkhani. "My purpose is to see the officer in charge of these fine troops."

Ignoring the transparent flattery, Laghari said, "I am in charge. What do you want?"

Hasni made his small half-bow again, then said, "My master sends me from Sanjrani to inform you that we have a stranger in our village. He speaks English, carries weapons. We have not seen him before."

Colonel Laghari felt his pulse quicken. An English-speaking stranger, armed! How could he not have some connection to the recent ambush.

"One stranger only?" he demanded, "How and why has he come to… What is your village called, again?"

"Sanjrani, sir. The stranger travels with a man well-known to us, whose family still lives among us. It is not our fault that he—"

"What is the other's name?" Laghari interrupted Hasni's clumsy effort to absolve himself, his village, of responsibility for sheltering a terrorist.

"Hussein Gorshani, sir," the youth replied. He stood with eyes downcast, hands clasped in front of him, as if to shield his groin.

"Those two, and no one else?" Laghari asked.

"No one," Hasni answered, adding "sir" in the nick of time.

"Why did they choose your village?"

"For Gorshani's family, perhaps, sir. Also, they have purchased ropes and other things for climbing mountains."

What?

That information seemed to make no sense. Why would they kill twelve soldiers, then prepare to scale a mountain? Were they lunatics?

Could two men even manage to surprise and kill a dozen soldiers, ten of them riding inside an APC? It seemed improbable, and yet…

Colonel Laghari faced Hasni and asked, "How far away is this Sanjrani?"

SLEEP WAS a luxury in Bolan's world. On missions, it was often hard to come by, sometimes nonexistent. He had long since learned to snatch the rare quiet moments whenever they were granted to him—or to sleep through hell's own racket, even standing up, until it threatened him.

Survival in the Executioner's world meant sleeping lightly and waking in a heartbeat, totally alert, ready to fight or flee. The meal of curry he'd enjoyed helped Bolan fall asleep, but it did not prevent him from snapping awake when a hand came to rest on his shoulder.

"It is only I," Gorshani said. His voice was strained by the pressure of Bolan's pistol, jammed beneath his chin.

Bolan withdrew the gun but did not holster it. His eyes scoured the small room that had been allotted to him.

"What's going on?" he inquired.

Grim-faced, Gorshani said, "There is a traitor in the village—Imran Hasni. May vultures pick his bones while he still lives."

"So, what's he done?"

"His oldest son has gone for soldiers, to inform them of us. The youngest of his children, little Lani, cannot bear her father's shame. She came and told my aunt."

Questions filled Bolan's mind, but he asked only two of them. "How far away's the nearest military base? How long has Hasni's boy been gone?"

"The nearest regular facility is in Mansehra, about eighty miles away. But Hasni's son went south. Mansehra lies off to the east."

Bolan was already on his feet when he said, "Maybe he

heard of a patrol nearby. They're hunting us right now. We knew they would be."

"Yes," Gorshani said. "But I did not expect them to be here so soon."

"They aren't here yet," Bolan reminded him. "The best way to protect your people is to make sure *we* aren't here when they arrive."

"Of course." Gorshani nodded. "We must go at once."

Their newly purchased climbing gear was already in the SUV waiting for them. Bolan hauled his military hardware to the car, while his companion said a quick round of good-byes to his aunt's family.

Once they were on the road, Bolan asked, "What happens to the rat?"

"Imran Hasni will die, but he will answer questions first. Of that, I have no doubt. As for his son, Mahmood…it's difficult to say. The Koran tells children to obey their fathers in all things, and yet… Well, who knows what will become of him?"

"Suppose the soldiers come expecting to meet Hasni? What happens if he's already dead?"

Gorshani frowned at that in the dashboard's faint light. "There will be interrogations," he replied. "Perhaps reprisals."

Bolan knew that tune.

In countries where the rule of law was often strained, at best—or even where it was embodied in a centuries-old code of laws—results were often valued over statutory prohibitions.

In fact, that was why Stony Man Farm existed.

"It's the middle of the night. Where did you plan on going?" he asked Gorshani.

"We shall find somewhere else to sleep," the driver said. "Perhaps a side road, where they cannot see us from the highway."

"And it's how far to the mountain we'll be climbing?"

"Eighty miles, approximately," Gorshani said.

Maybe an hour and a half, if the condition of the roads remained constant. And then add time on top of that, in the event they lost pavement during their approach to Mount Khakwani. Bolan's watch told him that it was barely midnight, placing sunrise five or six hours away.

Darkness was Bolan's friend—but only to a point. Gorshani couldn't drive without headlights on ancient, pot-holed roads, unless they wanted to risk damage ranging from flat tires to broken axles. And nocturnal travel in the North-West Frontier Province made them suspect at the best of times. Now, with a dozen soldiers dead and a determined manhunt underway, the less time they spent driving through the night, the better.

"Maybe," Bolan said, "we ought to turn around. See how your folks are doing with the army first before we split."

"The mission—"

"We're not climbing mountains in the dark," the Executioner said, interrupting the protest. "And camping at the mountain while we wait for sunrise doesn't strike me as the best idea."

"If we go back…"

"To have a look, is all," Bolan said. "Watch and learn."

"And when the soldiers leave…"

"We're on our way," Bolan confirmed. "Still ample time to cover eighty miles and hit the slopes."

Gorshani seemed to think about it for another quarter mile, then braked the SUV and cranked it through an awkward U-turn in the middle of the narrow road.

COLONEL LAGHARI let the other M113 APC directly follow Mahmood Hasni back toward Sanjrani, while his own vehicle trailed behind. One lesson he had learned from studying the ambush scene was that he did not wish to be in front if there was rocket fire, land mines, or any other deadly obstacles.

There was a chance, however slight, that Hasni had misled

him. The excursion to Sanjrani might turn out to be a trap, set by the same men who had massacred the first patrol. So far, Laghari had no inkling as to who the killers were, although the introduction of an English-speaking stranger argued against native bandits or guerrillas.

And there was the parachute, recovered by troops from Mansehra before Laghari arrived to command the investigation. He had believed it to be related to the killings, but Laghari could gather little more than the fact that the parachute was made for jumping, and not for cargo drops. Laghari also now assumed that it had belonged to their unknown English-speaker in Sanjrani.

Assuming that he existed.

Laghari clutched his submachine gun tightly, looking forward to the moment when the killers stood before him. If he found them in Sanjrani, then he would reward the Hasni family for helping him. If they escaped somehow, before his convoy reached the village, then Laghari would demand to know how it had happened.

But if this was some elaborate deception, organized to draw him off the scent—or worse, into a trap—Sanjrani's peasants would have much to answer for.

Laghari would not leave the village until he had learned the truth, whatever that might be. And anyone who lied to him, or tried to otherwise obstruct him, would have cause to rue the day that he was born.

IT WAS after midnight when the APCs finally rolled into Sanjrani, and fatigue was wearing on Laghari's nerves. He felt more irritable by the moment, less inclined to hear evasions or excuses. When he thought of Brigadier Bahaar Jadoon, relaxing at his villa in Rawalpindi, it only increased the agitation that he felt.

The APCs entered the village with their searchlights glaring, sweeping over shops and homes, probing the empty streets. Laghari ordered his driver to give the peasants a blast from the siren, knowing that its banshee wail would rouse even the soundest sleeper in Sanjrani. Moments later, when the people started straggling from their homes, Laghari ordered his men to dismount, then followed them into the night.

Laghari spoke Urdu and English—the latter still Pakistan's official language, despite the passage of six decades since the British occupation forces had departed—but he still required a translator for Pashto. In this case, he was relying on a corporal who'd volunteered to translate for him soon after Laghari had arrived in Peshawar. The man's name was Malik Tarkani, and he aimed to please.

Surveying glum and sleepy faces in the spotlight's glare, Laghari estimated that he had two-thirds of Sanjrani's peasants ranged before him. Others, he supposed, would not come out unless his soldiers went from door-to-door and dragged them from their hovels. For the moment, though, the colonel thought his audience was large enough.

"I want the chief or headman," he informed Tarkani. "Tell them."

As Tarkani translated, Laghari watched the faces change. No one seemed groggy now. Those who were not afraid looked angry and resentful at the rude disturbance of their sleep. That did not faze Laghari, since he had not come to win new friends.

The second time his translator repeated the instruction for Sanjrani's headman to identify himself, an aging character stepped forward, blinking under the harsh lights.

"Do you speak English?" Laghari asked. "Or Urdu?"

The old man nodded.

"Well? Which is it?"

"Some English," the old man said grudgingly.

"That's better. And are you in charge of this village?"

Now the old man shrugged. "I give advice, sometimes," he said. "I have no title, no salary."

"Is there another who outranks you, then?"

The bearded gnome considered it, then shook his head.

"I cannot hear you!" Laghari snarled.

"No, sir," the old man replied. If anything, his voice had grown softer.

"In that case," Laghari said, "you are just the man I want."

GORSHANI FELT something like panic churning inside him. It was a strange feeling, one he had not experienced since childhood, which increased his pulse rate, made him short of breath and caused a sickly churning in his stomach.

All for what?

The notion of a traitorous informer in Sanjrani sickened him, but he was not tremendously surprised. In any place where hundreds lived together, there would always be a certain fringe of malcontents, dissenters, troublemakers. Still, he'd never thought that any of the villagers he knew would stoop so low as to inform on his, Gorshani's, family.

Imran Hasni would pay for this night's work. Gorshani swore that promise to himself, adding the curt proviso, If I remain alive.

The tall American who called himself Matt Cooper—a cover name, no doubt—had never suggested that they act against the soldiers who had to certainly have reached Sanjrani by this time.

"To have a look, is all," he'd told Gorshani. "Watch and learn."

But if the soldiers proved too aggressive and violent, what, then? Was Gorshani expected to sit back and watch while his friends, his family, were abused?

"Two miles," he said, to help distract himself from ugly thoughts.

His passenger did not reply.

A mile from Sanjrani, when the glare of spotlights in the village was a mere bright speck, Gorshani killed the SUV's headlights and slowed his pace accordingly. He navigated by moonlight and memory, dodging the larger potholes and holding a speed that made the smaller ones manageable.

A half mile from the village, he began looking for a place where he could leave the vehicle. Gorshani recognized the lights and bustle that attended military occupation, and he knew it would be unwise to drive into that killing zone with the American beside him, and their weapons and equipment in the SUV.

"We should walk back from here," he said, as he turned off the two-lane blacktop onto dirt and gravel. It was an access road of sorts—or would have been if it lead anywhere.

"Suits me," Bolan told him, as the vehicle slowed to a halt.

Gorshani switched off the dome light before they opened the doors, a small detail that nonetheless he felt proud he'd thought of. Was pride a sin, according to the words of the Koran? Gorshani didn't think so, but if he was wrong, it had to be one of the lesser sins, entirely separate from murder and adultery.

Murder.

For that one, he would have to trust the Prophet's intercession with Allah to cleanse his soul.

"They should not see us if we go this way," he said, already whispering despite their distance from Sanjrani. "Watch for snakes."

"Thanks for the warning," Bolan said.

The moonlit landscape was completely alien. Although Gorshani had spent many nights with his mother's kinfolk in Sanjrani, no one from the village ever wandered far across the open land at night. It held too many dangers—asps and vipers, pitfalls, prowling jackals and cutthroats who would kill a man for pocket change or rape a woman first, before she died.

Night within most of the North-West Frontier Province

was strictly a time for sleeping, storing up one's energy to face another grueling day.

"I do not have binoculars," Gorshani suddenly announced, still whispering.

"I have a pair," Bolan replied. "Small ones, but adequate."

Gorshani nodded, relieved that his mistake would not further endanger them. Granted, he had not known they would be creeping around soldiers in the dark, but going off to hunt a group of madmen in the mountains should have prompted him to bring field glasses for surveillance anyway.

Covering the final hundred yards was the worst for Gorshani. He imagined that each slip and scrape of his feet on dry soil had to be audible in the village, forewarning the soldiers of his approach. Would they be waiting for him, with their weapons leveled, when he came into range?

Again, as if reading his mind, Bolan said, "They can't hear us. Not yet."

I hope not, Gorshani thought, as he crept up to the outskirts of Sanjrani, looking for a place to hide.

"THERE ARE NO strangers here," Sanjrani's headman told Colonel Laghari.

He was called Aban Gardezi, and the colonel did not trust a word he said.

"No strangers," Laghari said.

"None, sir."

"Would it then surprise you, if I said that someone in this village summoned us because you had two strangers hiding here, both armed, suspected of involvement in mass murder?"

"Yes, sir."

"Yes, what?"

"Yes, it would surprise me, sir."

"You know a man named Imran Hasni, of this village?" Laghari asked.

"I know everyone who lives here, sir."

"I'm asking about Imran Hasni, now."

"I know him, sir." Was that a flicker of disgust on Gardezi's face?

"Is he among the people standing with us here?"

The headman made a show of slowly turning, studying the faces that surrounded him, rising on tiptoe from time to time to examine faces in the rear of the assembled crowd.

At last, he turned to face Laghari once again and said, "I do not see him, sir."

"Is he a heavy sleeper?"

"How would I know, sir?"

"Produce him. Bring him here to me at once."

"Sir, I cannot invade another's home."

Laghari frowned, a thoughtful look, then said, "You're right. That's my job. Lead these soldiers to his house immediately. You, and you! You, too!" he barked at three privates. "Go with this man and bring Imran Hasni before me."

Without their headman present, Sanjrani's residents began to stir and mutter. They were more frightened than angry at the moment. Laghari was not worried. Each of his M113 had a .50-caliber machine gun trained on the crowd, capable of pouring out 600 rounds per minute.

At the first sign of a hostile movement from the crowd, Laghari simply had to shout one word, and all who stood before him would be shredded by a storm of armor-piercing bullets. Sanjrani would cease to exist as a viable community.

Colonel Laghari was still smiling at that mental image when his soldiers returned. One shoved Gardezi before him, while the other two half carried a body between them, its feet dragging limp on the ground.

They dropped the corpse in front of Laghari, one private reaching down to roll the dead man over, on his back. Beneath the spotlight's glare, Laghari saw the open throat, the shirt soaked through with crimson, showing other stab wounds lower down.

"Is this Imran Hasni?" Laghari asked the village headman.

"It appears so, sir."

"Is it, or is it not?" Laghari shouted in the old man's face. Unflinching, he replied, "It is, sir."

"Can you tell me who killed him?" Laghari asked.

"No, sir," Gardezi answered. "I saw nothing."

"And I suppose the others saw that same nothing?"

The headman shrugged. "I speak for no one but myself, sir."

"On the contrary," Laghari said. "You represent the village."

"Not in this, sir."

"Well, then, can you guess who might have done this thing? Who hated him enough to gut him like a sheep at slaughter?"

"No, sir."

"But you agree that someone must know something."

"Who can say, sir?"

"You leave me no choice," the colonel said. "I am compelled, now, to interrogate each person in this village, man and woman, old and young. No one shall rest until the truth is known to me."

"As you command, sir."

Addressing the soldier who had led the three-man party to the dead man's home, Laghari asked, "Who else was in the house?"

"No one, sir."

Turning back to Gardezi, he said, "I know this Hasni had a son. Is there a wife, as well? More children?"

"He does, sir," the headman replied.

"So, where are they?" Laghari demanded.

"I have no idea, sir."

"Indeed? Then it appears that I must help you run your village," the colonel said. Turning to his soldiers, Laghari made a sweeping gesture with one arm, shouting, "You lot! And you, there! I want ten two-man teams. Search the village, house by house. Bring any stragglers forward, and subdue those who resist. I will resume interrogation when I have Imran Hasni's wife and children before me. Now, go!"

His men broke ranks, formed pairs and pushed off through the crowd. Laghari kept his place between the APCs, covered by twin machine guns, flanked by his lieutenant and the APC drivers, all armed with rifles. His submachine gun's weight felt reassuring in his hands.

He would have answers soon. Answers about the strangers who were either hidden in Sanjrani or had passed this way, and answers about the murder of Imran Hasni. If Hasni's wife and other children had been slain, as well, Laghari thought he might as well arrest the whole damned village for complicity in murder, let the courts and lawyers sort it out.

But he *would* have his answers.

Soon.

7

Bolan knew Sanjrani's headman was in trouble as soon as he'd seen the blood-smeared corpse. His Steiner 7x50 Commander III binoculars revealed the scene in stark relief, almost as if he stood right beside the Pakistani officer who stared down at the body.

Bolan passed the glasses to Gorshani, saying, "That must be your squealer."

Bolan's guide surveyed the scene, frowning, and handed back the glasses. "Imran Hasni," he said. "They should have waited."

Or have been quicker to remove the body, Bolan thought.

It was a hard call, either way. Letting the turncoat live, with soldiers on the way, risked having him do even more damage than he'd already done. Slitting his throat, without disposing of the evidence, left someone—maybe the whole village—subject to a murder prosecution under Pakistani law, which ranked among the world's most controversial legal systems.

Downrange, the officer in charge was pacing back and forth in front of his captive audience, nearly stepping on the corpse of Imran Hasni as he waved his arms, haranguing the villagers. He seemed to be making a speech of some kind, though Bolan couldn't hear or translate what he said.

"I need to get down there," he told Gorshani. "If it falls apart, I want to be closer. You coming?"

"Yes," his driver said without a heartbeat's hesitation.

Bolan had no plan in mind as he began his scuttling

advance under cover of darkness. Spotlights mounted on the APCs blinded the villagers who might have seen him and Gorshani coming otherwise, while all the soldiers faced inward, their weapons covering the crowd. The officer's raised voice and the idling engines of his vehicles covered whatever sounds the two advancing shadow warriors made.

The very last thing Bolan wanted was another clash with Pakistani troops, burning up time and ammunition, leaving bodies in his wake, and risking death before he even reached his mission's destination. He wouldn't intervene in any kind of orderly arrest, but if it went the other way...

One problem flashing through his mind arose from simple math. He knew the M113 APCs seated two crewmen and eleven passengers apiece. His head count of the soldiers present told him that the vehicles were full, meaning that they could take a maximum of one or two prisoners each, packed in like sardines, if they sat on the floor near each APC's rear exit hatch.

For any larger roundup, the officer in charge would have to phone or radio for trucks to haul the prisoners away. That meant a wait of several hours, while the convoy formed in Peshawar and wound its way to Sanjrani. It would be dawn before the reinforcements got there, even if they started getting organized immediately.

Bolan couldn't afford to watch and wait that long—nor, from the sound of his ongoing tirade, was the Pakistani officer a fellow long on patience. Anything he planned to do would happen soon, in Bolan's estimation, and it didn't sound like he was in a mood for legal niceties.

Suddenly the officer stopped short before the village headman, bellowing a question at him. When the chief made his inaudible reply, the officer lashed out with force enough to break the old man's nose and knock him off his feet.

"Not yet," Bolan gritted to Gorshani at his side.

It might end there, with an arrest, if they were lucky.

Bolan might have actually crossed his fingers if his hands weren't wrapped around the pistol grips of his assault rifle and its grenade launcher, with index fingers curled around their triggers.

Ready for some fool to ring the doorbell at the gates of hell.

COLONEL LAGHARI felt a sudden, heady rush of power as he slammed his clenched fist into the headman's face. He felt the nasal cartilage implode and watched the old man drop, groaning, shaking his head to clear it.

"Murder is a capital offense!" he shouted at the peasants facing him beneath the glare of spotlights. "Convicted killers may be hanged, or shot by firing squad."

He let those words sink in, saw peasants stirring in the crowd, exchanging nervous glances while their chief squirmed on the ground in front of them. When he believed they'd had enough time to consider death, Laghari spoke again.

"In cases such as this—" he waved a hand toward Imran Hasni's cooling corpse "—one man or woman may not bear the penalty alone. Protecting enemies of Pakistan and lying to investigators in a case of national security are crimes against the state. They also make offenders subject to the punishment of death."

Again, he paused, pleased by the murmuring he heard, although he dared not smile.

"Perhaps only one person stabbed this man," Laghari said. "But he, the victim, was assisting us, your country's sworn defenders, in pursuit of enemies who have already killed twelve soldiers and are plainly bent on terrorist activity against the state. Those who protect the murderers, by action or by silence, share their guilt. And I can promise you that those who do not help us now will share the killers' punishment also."

The muttering had ended now. Laghari thought the faces of

the villagers had hardened, somehow, while he spoke. Instead of being frightened, they now seemed angry. For an instant, he was worried that they might attack and overwhelm him, then he thought of the machine guns mounted on his APCs, the rifles leveled by his soldiers and the SMG in his own hands.

There was no danger here, except to those who actively opposed his will.

"Who will identify the slayers of this man?" he asked the crowd.

A ringing silence answered him. No voice or hand was raised.

"Where are the victim's wife and children?" he demanded. Nothing.

Laghari had grown up on jokes about the archetypal village idiot, but never in his life had he imagined a community where *all* the occupants were idiots.

How else could he explain their stubbornness?

His rage boiled over, surging through Laghari's veins. If he permitted such defiance by a clutch of worthless peasants, how could he pretend to be a military leader worthy of his rank, much less promotion?

"You leave me no choice," he told Sanjrani's residents. "Each person here is guilty by association, both of murder and of crimes against the state. I call upon you to surrender."

As he spoke, Laghari raised his left hand, whipped it in a tight circle that told his two machine gunners to find their marks and hold their weapons steady. If he spiked his thumb, then dropped his arm, the .50-calibers would blaze away.

Giddy with excitement now, Laghari barked, "I say again—surrender! Your defiance of a lawful order leaves me no alternative but deadly force!"

The peasants looked confused and frightened now. Neither emotion would protect them.

Feeling almost godlike in that frozen moment, Laghari raised his rigid thumb on high, where both machine gunners would see it, while he clutched his SMG in a one-handed grip.

Another second, and—

The first explosion's shock wave knocked him sprawling in the dust, his back peppered with shrapnel, burning as if half a dozen giant wasps had stung him, all at once.

IT WAS A CLOSE CALL at the final moment. Bolan had considered taking out the officer in charge, a clean shot from behind, but knew that might touch off a deadly firestorm from the two heavy machine guns mounted on the APCs. And that, in turn, would set the other soldiers firing their Kalashnikovs into the crowd.

He used the GP-25 instead, launching a 40 mm high-explosive round toward the nearest APC machine gunner. Bolan was up and moving by the time it blew, stunning the troops and villagers alike, drenching the nearest ranks with crimson rain.

Bolan gave no thought to Gorshani as he rushed the killing ground. Gorshani had been translating the officer's commands right up until the moment Bolan fired. The man's words had made it clear that there was no way to prevent a massacre of innocents without armed intervention. Now that it was happening, the guide was on his own.

Like Bolan.

Every soldier for himself.

Bolan's first priority was putting the remaining .50-caliber machine gun out of commission. Whether it stitched the fleeing villagers or swung around to face him, it was the deadliest weapon in play at the moment.

He hit the Pakistani gunner with a 3-round burst, just as the big M2 had begun to hammer death downrange. More screaming from the crowd could mean either someone was hit, or they were simply panicked by the gunfire. Whatever the situation, Bolan knew the only way that he could help them was by taking out the other troops.

Who, at the moment, seemed completely, utterly confused.

A few of them—six or seven, of the twenty-odd remaining soldiers—fired short bursts at the retreating peasants, probably believing that some member of the village crowd had tossed a hand grenade. It was the kind of mix-up that occurred with numbing regularity in combat, damned by critics, rarely prosecuted as a war crime, frequently relived in nightmares by survivors on both sides.

The trick was stopping it before the carnage spread.

And that, as Bolan knew, meant drawing fire upon himself.

He found a gap between the idling APCs and squeezed off two short bursts that dropped three uniforms like sacks of rumpled, dirty laundry on the ground. Instead of taking down the men on either side of the fallen soldiers, he hesitated long enough to let them turn and glimpse him, and then predictably shout to alert their comrades as they scrambled in pursuit.

And now Bolan hit the sticky part of his impromptu plan.

Having revealed himself to armed men who would surely try to kill him, how would he stay alive?

He fed the GP-25 another HE round and turned to face the soldiers who suddenly came charging through the gap between the APCs. Crouching, Bolan triggered it, then stitched the posse's leader with a rising burst before the frag grenade's blast swept the rest of them away.

So far, so good.

More crackling fire beyond the smoky haze, and spotlights told him that Gorshani had to have joined the fight. Bolan could only wish him well at that point, and continue fighting to survive.

Suddenly he had an idea, and quickly translated it to action as he scrambled for the closest APC. He found a hand grip, vaulted to the fender, then mounted the turret, scuttling toward the .50-caliber M2.

A dead man was slumped over the gun's spade grips. Bolan easily hauled him clear and jammed him inside the open hatch, which had failed to save him moments earlier. The body crumpled, dropping out of sight, as Bolan took his place behind the gun.

GORSHANI COULDN'T keep up with Matt Cooper in a footrace toward the armored vehicles. The tall American was stronger and faster. Rather than wind up limp and gasping at the finish line, Gorshani struck his own course, veering off from the other man's track and pounding toward a shallow swale that ran along the east side of Sanjrani.

If he reached it, he would have sparse cover but also a field of fire that included roughly half the soldiers standing near the closer APC. It would be easy for the turret gunner to pivot and kill him, but Gorshani figured that if he shot that soldier first—

But before that thought was fully formed, Cooper seemed to have plucked it from his skull and claimed it for his own. The tall man triggered one of his grenades and sent a fireball leaping from the turret of the APC Gorshani had meant to target himself. The flash narrowed Gorshani's eyes, while its concussion swept him with a bitter, smoky wind.

Gorshani ducked and rolled, feeling a needle-lance of pain as shrapnel grazed his left thigh. Sliding face-first into cover, he stayed down just long enough to clear his head, then popped back up again, his AKMS rifle shouldered, seeking targets.

The explosion had changed everything.

Gorshani felt as if he was in a trance as he watched the scene before him. Before its echo had died, most of the soldiers had begun to fire upon Sanjrani villagers, who in turn, had broken their formation and were now fleeing for their lives. Gorshani saw some of them lurch and fall as they were hit, but others ducked and crawled beneath the stream of fire, or sprinted for the cover of adjacent homes.

Then Gorshani noticed Cooper, thirty yards off to his left,

firing short bursts from his rifle. This action seemed to break his spell, releasing Gorshani to join the fight. Some of his people were escaping, were surviving, and he had to help them if he could.

Gorshani found his first mark close at hand, a young soldier retreating in a crab-walk to the cover of the APC's blunt nose. He had no inkling of an enemy behind him, and Gorshani gave no warning, simply shot him once between the shoulder blades and dropped him facedown in the sand.

How many more remained?

He had stopped counting at twenty, when he saw Cooper make his rush to meet the enemy. Gorshani seemed to recall that this model of APC carried thirteen men, but his memory could have been faulty.

Whatever the total, the big American had killed at least one with his first shot, shredding the turret machine gunner who might have otherwise slain half the villagers present—or turned on Gorshani and riddled him on the spot, in his ditch.

Who next?

The soldiers who'd been visible before Cooper fired his grenade were crouched and hiding now. Gorshani could no longer see them, much less reach them with his bullets, unless he left cover and moved out onto the open killing ground.

He had been about to risk it, when two men in uniform appeared before him, jogging toward the nearest of Sanjrani's dwellings in pursuit of fleeing villagers. One fired a short burst from the hip and sent a woman tumbling, screaming, to the ground.

Gorshani shot that soldier, nothing but cold rage in his heart as he squeezed off two rounds in semiauto rapid-fire. The first was high and clipped the soldier's helmet, sending it flying, knocking him off balance. That, in turn, threw off Gorshani's second shot, but it was not entirely ruined. He saw blood spray from the soldier's lower face, perhaps a mouth wound, as the man went down.

Gorshani tracked around to find the second soldier, and framed him in his sights, just as the man heard his partner's cry of pain and was turning to see what had befallen him. Gorshani's fourth shot of the battle drilled the soldier's left cheek, snapped his head backward and took out a palm-sized fragment of his skull as it exited.

Meanwhile, the enemy with the face wound had dropped to all fours, groping around for his weapon while blood drizzled from torn lips. Gorshani couldn't stand to watch him any longer, so he fired a mercy round into the wounded soldier's scalp and put him down.

COLONEL LAGHARI took a moment to remember who and where he was. The simple act of drawing breath took painful effort, but Laghari could not say if he was actually wounded, or if he'd merely had the wind knocked out of him by the close-range explosion.

It all came back to him within a second and a half.

Sanjrani. Grilling the headman. The discovery of Imran Hasni's mutilated corpse. Laghari's judgment rendered on the village populace. And then—

The hammering of automatic weapons told him that the blast that felled him was no accident. A rocket? Were they under fire by rebels? Had one of Sanjrani's peasants squirreled away a hand grenade?

Laghari was surprised to find that he still clutched his submachine gun. Training paid off—or pure survival instinct?

The colonel struggled to his knees and was about to stand, when he decided that wouldn't be wise with so many weapons blazing all around him. Though he saw no one but his own soldiers firing at the moment, he knew that proved nothing. He also knew they would not hear him, even if he gave the cease-fire order.

He'd have to reach one of the APCs and get inside, where

it was safe, to use the built-in PA system. Then his men would hear and recognize his voice, and they would obey.

Laghari started crawling, staying low, flinching when bullets struck the armored flank of the hulking vehicle beside him. Was it sniper fire, or stray rounds from his panicked men?

Laghari didn't know—and, at the moment, didn't care.

The most important thing, right now, was reaching safety. Once inside the ACP, he could survey the field through periscopes, seek hostile gunmen in the shadows, and redirect the spotlights, if need be, to help his men find targets.

And if there were no opponents to be slain, he could command a momentary cease-fire, then rally his remaining troops to sweep Sanjrani clean of human life.

Laghari knew the village harbored traitors to the government. He'd lost his chance to question them about the parachuting stranger and the murder of a dozen soldiers earlier that day—no, yesterday actually, since it was past midnight— but he could still exact revenge.

And in the process, he could silence any inconvenient witnesses who might seek to destroy his promising career.

When he eventually reported this engagement to the officer in charge at Peshawar, and then to Brigadier Bahaar Jadoon, he would describe it as a battle with insurgents. Thanks to Allah, he had casualties and damage to the APCs that would support his claim. There need be no mention of a threat to annihilate Sanjrani's villagers because they would not talk.

Reaching the gap between the APCs, Laghari rose at last on cramping legs, reached for the nearest handhold on the second vehicle, and dragged himself laboriously toward the hatch on top. From there, unless a bullet found him, he could simply slide through the hatch and make himself secure inside the armored shell.

Laghari reached the summit of the APC and froze, staring

at the stranger crouched behind the .50-caliber machine gun. Who was this? What did it mean?

All questions vanished from his mind as the intruder swung the forty-four-inch barrel to his right, and trained its gaping muzzle on Laghari's face.

UNLIKE THE .44 Magnum pistol immortalized by Hollywood, the Browning M2 .50-caliber machine gun really *was* powerful enough to blow a human head clean off—and when Bolan thumbed down the butterfly trigger, it did precisely that.

The Pakistani colonel didn't even have a chance to scream before his skull was vaporized by 647-grain bullets traveling at 3,044 feet per second, meeting flesh and bone with 13,144 foot-pounds of destructive energy. The headless body fell away, and Bolan swung the M2 back around toward the patrol's remaining soldiers.

It was commonplace to say that men cut down in combat never knew what hit them, and that was precisely true for some of those whom Bolan strafed with the Browning M2, firing short bursts to conserve ammunition at the standard cyclic rate of 600 rounds per minute. Those who were not facing Bolan when he found them likely felt only an instant's stunning pain, as bullets meant to pierce armor shredded their flesh and bones. They dropped like puppets with their strings cut, rarely making any sound beyond the thud of their bodies striking the earth.

But others definitely saw it coming, knew exactly what was happening—even if they could not grasp how or why it was happening. Those who'd seen their comrades cut down from behind and turned to see what madness had possessed the friendly turret gunner gaped in shock or cursed before they died. Some bolted; others stood their ground, returning fire.

Each man's death was his own. He may not choose the time or place, he may not even realize that he was dying, but no two departures from this life were ever perfectly identical.

Each man had to ultimately die alone.

And so it was for these.

The Executioner claimed each of them in turn, sweeping his scythe from left to right and back again, across the killing field. He felt no more or less for those who died with their backs turned, or running hopelessly for cover, than he did for those who spent their final seconds bent on killing him.

Surprise, shifting to full-blown panic in a heartbeat, spoiled the aim of those who threatened Bolan. He heard their bullets rattle past him, even felt a couple of them go by, and grimaced as one lucky ricochet plucked at his sleeve, missing the flesh beneath. And all the while, his Browning hammered at them, spewing four-inch casings, mulching flesh and bone with bullets flying half a mile per second.

At the last instant, two of the soldiers almost escaped.

Almost.

They had sprinted out of Bolan's view, around the nose of the first APC, where he could neither track nor drop them. The Executioner was ready to dismount and follow them, root them out and drop them with his rifle—or by hand, if that was what it took—when both came reeling back, twitching and jerking through a clumsy death dance.

Bolan saw the bullets rip into their bodies, heard the crack-crack-crack of a Kalashnikov in semiauto mode, and then watched Gorshani step from hiding, firing two more rounds before the dying soldiers fell.

One of the fallen men was still moving, perhaps without conscious volition, but Gorshani swiftly ended it. He stepped in close, bent and pressed the muzzle of his AKMS to the wounded soldier's forehead, triggering a point-blank mercy round.

"That's all, I think," he called to Bolan from the ground below the APCs.

He had it right. No enemies remained in need of killing. It was time to see how many friendlies had been slain or wounded in the short, chaotic firefight—and to also learn if they were still friendlies.

Bolan dismounted from the APC and joined Gorshani on the field of death.

8

Islamabad

The martyr's name was Sabeir Hamayun. He was originally from Taloqan, Afghanistan, and on his next birthday he would have been eighteen years old.

The fact that he would never see that birthday did not frighten Hamayun. He had been chosen for a sacred role in the jihad and promised entry into Paradise, with all its wonders, if he played his part successfully.

He'd been told that Allah judged the intent of martyrs and did not weigh success in earthly, human terms. It would not matter, therefore, if he failed to kill huge numbers of demonic infidels this day.

Those who survived his sacrifice would fall another day, when yet another martyr was dispatched to strike in Allah's name.

His target was the same Crusader church whose leaders had stubbornly refused to heed the message that they were not welcome here. The very name Islamabad should have alerted them to this truth. If that was not enough, they only needed to consult a map, to see that they were laboring in vain. How could their faith take root in the *Islamic* Republic of Pakistan?

Were mosques permitted in the Holy See of Rome? Were Torahs found in Shinto shrines?

The very thought was ludicrous!

Hamayun walked along Shah Abdul Latif Bhitai Road,

past shops and market stalls, eastbound toward Sachal Sarmast Road. Before he reached that second major artery, he would turn left—or north—into the side street where his target was located.

Everything had been arranged to let him strike with maximum effect. His sacrifice was timed to precede worship services, when the Crusaders would be on their way to church, some of them running late and hurrying to get there, others idling on the steps and sidewalks, making small talk.

None of them would recognize him. Hamayun had been sequestered from the time he was delivered to Islamabad, his only knowledge of its streets drawn from the maps he'd studied and a brief glimpse caught as he was hustled from a closed van to the front door of the safehouse where he'd spent the last week of his life. His only contacts in the city had been a group of fellow Shiites who had catered to his every need and prayed for his success.

The hidden vest he wore, bearing its blocks of Semtex A, with plastic bags of dung and shrapnel, weighed nineteen kilos. Hamayun had practiced wearing it for six nights past, learning to walk without betraying his concealed burden. He'd imagined that the walking lessons were like those absorbed by Western "super models" in their filthy glamour schools—except that Hamayun was learning how to save souls, not corrupt them and entice them to damnation.

Now that he was on his own, unsupervised, it was surprising that the deadly vest felt so light on his shoulders. Hamayun was not an athlete—far from it, in fact. Back in Afghanistan, he'd been a bookish child who shied away from sports, even before the Taliban had seized control of Taloqan and banned most decadent amusements.

Still, the nineteen kilos—nearly forty pounds—seemed to weigh almost nothing as he moved along the crowded sidewalk. Though Hamayun knew he was walking, his buoyancy of spirit made it feel like levitation. If he floated any higher, he imagined, he could look down on the people passing by him, busy with their own pursuits, oblivious to his exalted mission.

Most of them were Muslims, he assumed.

Hamayun hoped those would be spared—but if they fell and if their souls were clean, they had nothing to fear.

He found the side street, recognized its name and saw the workmen sweating over picks and jackhammers. Their foreman seemed to spend more time watching the foot traffic on Shah Abdul Latif Bhitai Road than he did supervising his men, dark eyes beneath his turban flicking over faces as they passed.

Those eyes met Hamayun's and hesitated for an instant, then moved on. No risk of interference with his mission there.

The detonator button dangled from a wire inside the right sleeve of Hamayun's robe, clutched in the hand he kept inside his pocket. His instructions for the detonation had been simple: wait until he reached the sidewalk outside the Crusader church, then press the button once to arm it. When his thumb mashed down a second time, the Semtex would explode.

And Hamayun would feel no pain. It had been promised to him, time and time again. Of course, his body would be shredded by the blast, but that would be over in an instant. He supposed that it would be like falling on his head and being knocked unconscious, then awakening brief moments later at the gates of Paradise.

And, oh, what rewards awaited him!

Hamayun felt himself begin to stiffen at the thought of forty virgins, servile to his every whim, eternally anxious to please. Was sexual exhaustion possible in Paradise, where everyone was young, healthy and vigorous until the end of time?

The young man passed the barricades erected by the laborers, as if a gap had been deliberately left for him. The foreman looked away, perhaps distracted by some passing vehicle. The church lay half a block ahead, on Hamayun's right.

It was exactly as it had been described during his briefings. The Crusaders milled about outside, chatting and laughing, as if they had every right to soil the sidewalks of Islamabad. Allowed to spread unchecked, they might lure thousands from the One True Faith and steal their souls from Allah.

Hamayun was smiling as he moved among them, hearing their voices without absorbing a word that was spoken. He found his place, midsidewalk, near the steps that served their church. Such crowded steps.

He pressed the detonator button once, mouthing a short prayer of his own, and then again, putting his soul to flight.

Hamayun never heard the street fill up with screams.

Rawalpindi

BRIGADIER BAHAAR Jadoon sat at his desk, watching the grim news from Islamabad on PTV News, one of the channels broadcast by the state-owned Pakistan Television Network. He had the sound turned low on his imported Sony nineteen-inch TV, ignoring most of what was said by the reporters on the scene and so-called anchors in the studio.

The images attracted and repulsed Jadoon. Knowing that he had played a role in the disaster—had, in fact, been its facilitator—made him feel…what was the word he sought?

Definitely not proud.

Nor queasy.

Numb.

It struck him, in that instant, that he had no feeling for the victims of the blast, whether their deaths and mutilation had been planned or incidental. It was simply done.

Some measure of his vast debt to al Qaeda had been repaid.

Of course, Jadoon knew he would never be released from that grim obligation. He would never claim the mortgage papers on his soul—strike a match and watch them flare, then curl and crumble into ash.

Some obligations were eternal.

When the phone rang, Brigadier Jadoon was not surprised. He'd fielded several calls already, from superiors demanding action and subordinates requesting his advice on how to cope with the emergency. He had responded properly in each and every case, performing as if he shared their surprise at yet another act of terrorism in the nation's capital.

"Jadoon," he said to the receiver's mouthpiece.

"Sir," the unfamiliar voice came back at him, "I am Colonel Usama Bhel, assigned to army headquarters in Peshawar."

"What is it, Colonel?"

"Sir, I am afraid I have bad news."

"I know," Jadoon replied. "I'm watching it right now."

"Sorry? What do you mean, sir?"

"The explosion in Islamabad," he said, already losing patience with this stranger who was clearly simpleminded.

"Ah, yes, sir. But I'm afraid that bad news is not *my* bad news."

Frowning, Jadoon turned from the television set and said, "In that case, Colonel, please explain."

"Sir, I am calling to inform you that your emissary, Colonel Salim Laghari, has been killed in battle. At a village called Sanjrani, sir. With twenty-five good men."

"What did you say? Laghari's dead? In battle?"

"It appears there was some sort of ambush, sir. The colonel's unit was annihilated. Several peasants from the village also died. Naturally, there will be a full investigation."

"I plan to participate," Jadoon replied.

"Sir?"

"I will be sending some of my most trusted officers and men to help with your investigation, Colonel."

"Yes, sir. As you wish, sir."

"And I expect to be informed of any evidence that is discovered, as you find it."

"Absolutely, Brigadier."

"In that case, carry on." And with that the brigadier ended the conversation.

Jadoon cradled the telephone receiver, flicked his gaze back toward the television screen, then scooped up his remote control and switched it off.

Laghari, dead!

Jadoon had wanted to be rid of him, if only for a while, but he had not intended the assignment to the North-West Frontier Province as a death sentence. It seemed impossible, despite the recent massacre of soldiers he had sent Laghari to investigate.

But, then again…

Bahaar Jadoon already felt his shock receding, mellowing. Becoming, what? Relief? Pure joy?

He had despised Laghari—worse, had marked him as a spy intent on subverting Jadoon's rightful authority—so why should he now mourn the man's passing?

Of course, he'd be required to make the standard noises, voicing outrage at the loss of a valued subordinate, attending the full-dress military funeral where men who'd never met Salim Laghari would sing his posthumous praises.

What hypocrites they were! And yet, Jadoon was well acquainted with the politics involved behind the scenes, in every phase of military life. As much was done for show, as to achieve some verified, legitimate objective. No man reached the rank of brigadier without learning to play the game.

Jadoon's first move, regardless of his feelings toward Salim Laghari as a corpse or living man, had to be to seek the criminals responsible for killing possibly forty-six soldiers within a single day. The North-West Frontier Province had not seen such frantic action since the early days of the American invasion in Afghanistan.

Jadoon would have to not only appear to hunt the killers, but also find, identify and crush them if he wished to keep his present post, much less advance to higher rank. Such a flagrant challenge to authority, whether by rebels or apolitical outlaws, could not go unpunished.

Snatching up the telephone once more, he first summoned Lieutenant Colonel Raheem Davi. Next, Jadoon began to sketch the outlines of a campaign strategy inside his head.

He would field troops to find the men responsible for slaughtering his soldiers, but at the same time had to be cautious not to trespass on preserves claimed by al Qaeda. Jadoon dared not risk the exposure of his blood debt to al Qaeda, or the work that he had done on its behalf. Such revelations would not only finish his career in uniform, but also undoubtedly send him to the gallows.

Still, the brigadier was not overly concerned about his public mission clashing with his secret life. There was no reason to believe that soldiers of al Qaeda had killed his men. Why would they, when the Pakistani army made no effort to oppose Akram Ben Abd al-Bari and his kind?

Declaring war against the military would be tantamount to suicide, fouling the nest al-Bari and his aides relied upon for sanctuary.

No.

The men Jadoon was hunting now had to be of another breed entirely.

And if he succeeded in identifying them, that breed would soon become extinct.

IT WAS THE BEST part of an hour's work, loading the APCs with bloody corpses and discarded weapons. By the time they finished, there were twenty-seven bodies stacked inside the two vehicles, with Imran Hasni's included. Those who'd fallen in the village would be buried there, and Bolan left their handling—as well as the care of any wounded—to Sanjrani's grim survivors.

It was always difficult to take a reading from impassive faces, but the villagers seemed more resigned than angry over what had happened. Any who resented Bolan's intervention looked to the headman for their cue, and pitched in with the rest to put their village back in seminormal condition.

Bolan didn't know what kind of CSI techniques were used in Pakistan. No doubt, the army could discover that a skirmish had been fought here, at Sanjrani, but beyond that he had no idea. If experts tested every weapon carried by the soldiers, they would find that some were killed with other AKMS rifles, similar but not identical to those retrieved. They'd also determine that the rest were taken down by shrapnel and the .50-caliber Browning M2 mounted on one of their own APCs.

Bolan wasn't concerned about such things as hair and fiber samples, fingerprints, or DNA. His prints had been removed from every law enforcement file that mattered after he was "killed" in New York City, years before, and no lab could match any other form of evidence unless he was arrested and forced to provide samples.

That, he knew, would never happen.

So, the plan was relatively simple: load the APCs and drive them far enough away so that, when they were found, the finger of suspicion did not point immediately to Sanjrani. Let Military Intelligence or the Federal Investigation Agency work out what had happened. By the time they started grilling suspects, Bolan would be done with Pakistan.

One way or another.

By the time both APCs were loaded to capacity, Bolan had learned that only half a dozen of Sanjrani's residents knew how to drive, and none of them had ever driven heavy vehicles. Gorshani reckoned he could drive one APC, if Bolan took the other, but that left the problem of their SUV and how they would retrieve it from the village.

The headman solved that problem, saying he would follow in Gorshani's Mahindra Bolero, while one of the villagers trailed him on an ancient motorcycle that served Sanjrani as a form of community transport. That decided, Bolan left

Gorshani to his farewells and prepared to put the village behind him forever.

The APCs had no ignition keys. Like military vehicles the world over, push starters kept them mobile in emergencies when tiny, fragile things like keys could be easily broken, lost, stolen, or blown away. The Detroit Diesel 6V53T engine turned over at once and sat grumbling patiently while Bolan waited for Gorshani to fire up his own.

At last, the strange little convoy was moving. Bolan was in the lead, with Gorshani's APC behind him, followed by the SUV with the headman driving, and a skinny teenager bringing up the rear on a puttering two-wheeler. They drove six miles from the village, Bolan counting every yard of it on his odometer and hoping that they wouldn't meet another military unit headed in the opposite direction. He was not prepared to answer any questions on the radio, much less engage in face-to-face debate.

He chose a spot where flooding had created a wide gully on the west side of the road and nosed his APC into it. The M113's treads provided good traction all the way, and Bolan crawled along the gully for a hundred yards before he stopped and killed the engine. Gorshani pulled up close behind him, shutting down his engine and lights.

Bolan had found thermite grenades inside the APC and instantly made an adjustment to his plan. Instead of simply leaving the vehicles with their loads of carrion, he would incinerate them, thereby rendering whatever tests the army sought to carry out that much more difficult—perhaps impossible.

"I'm scorching them," he told Gorshani, holding up the two grenades by way of explanation. "You've got time for one more *alwidaa*."

"Farewell," Gorshani echoed. "Are you learning Urdu, Mr. Cooper?"

"You just heard my whole vocabulary."

"I'll be waiting in the car," Gorshani said, and turned away.

Bolan primed one grenade and dropped it through the open turret hatch of the APC he'd driven from Sanjrani, then repeated that procedure with the second vehicle. He was retreating at double-time when the first grenade detonated, smoke and white-hot light pouring from every vent and viewing slit the APC had. Inside, the pyrotechnic combination of aluminum powder and metal oxide would have produced temperatures approaching 4,500° Fahrenheit—nearly twice the melting point of steel.

Test that, he thought, as he was climbing from the gully to the road bed where Gorshani stood watching the motorcycle's taillights dwindling in the night.

"They'll be all right, if they keep quiet," Bolan told him, hoping it was true.

"I think so," Gorshani said, evidently joining in the wishful-thinking game.

"Think you can sleep?" he asked his guide. "It's pushing three o'clock."

"Two hours until sunrise," Gorshani said. "We had planned to leave Sanjrani by this time, in any case."

"So, right on time, then," Bolan said. "Let's hit the road."

Mount Khakwani, North-West Frontier Province

AKRAM BEN ABD al-Bari raised his bearded chin, the nod barely perceptible, but the guard saw it, bowed in response, and went off to fetch the unexpected visitor.

Someone had come calling at al-Bari's cave without an invitation. That the man was still alive meant he was one of only twenty-five or so on Earth who had been favored with the knowledge of al-Bari's whereabouts. The fact that he risked pleading for a brief, unscheduled audience meant that his business had to be urgent.

It had better be, al-Bari thought.

If someone had disturbed his slumber for some reason he

did not deem extremely urgent, then there would soon be one less person on the planet who could find his hideaway.

The guard returned a moment later with the visitor. Al-Bari recognized him instantly, of course. The caller was Karim Faisal, a comrade from the struggle in Afghanistan. His hair had more gray in it that al-Bari remembered, and Faisal's visage was grave.

"Forgive me for disturbing you," he said. "I tried to reach Arzou—"

"He is preoccupied," al-Bari said.

"Of course. Yet I believed that you should hear the news without delay."

"What news?"

"A military search is under way throughout the province," Faisal said, "seeking the men who ambushed a patrol and executed twenty soldiers."

"We were not involved," al-Bari said with perfect confidence. His warriors might occasionally think for themselves, but they only did what they were told.

"No, sir. But if the search continues, moving northward, they may ultimately reach this place."

"I think that you will find they are currently distracted in Islamabad."

Faisal blinked, drawing the connection, but he did not smile. "Perhaps, sir. But if any more soldiers are killed, it may be necessary for…for you…"

"Say it."

"To leave and find another headquarters."

"I think it shall not come to that."

Al-Bari did not plan to share the secret of his ties to Brigadier Jadoon. He recognized Faisal's concern, and while it was appreciated, he believed it was misplaced.

However, if the Pakistani army was engaged in sweeps throughout the province, seeking criminals or rebels, it *could* interrupt al-Bari's channels of communication with his agents

in Islamabad and Rawalpindi. He would have to be more cir-
cumspect than ever, until things were normalized once more.

"Thank you for the warning, Faisal. It was good of you to
come so far, with our best interest foremost in your heart. Our
victory is possible because of stalwart comrades such as you."

Faisal bowed deeply, his turban grazing the rug on which
he knelt. "I live only to serve in Allah's cause," he said.

"And you shall be rewarded, in this life or in the next."

"*As-Salamu Alaykum,*" Faisal said.

"*Alaykum As-Salaam,*" al-Bari replied.

Faisal retreated, vanishing through the hanging curtain
where a guard would meet him and escort him from the cave.
Al-Bari turned to one of his remaining sentries, saying, "Fetch
Ra'id Ibn Rashad."

The guard obeyed at once. The better part of ten minutes
elapsed before Rashad appeared, his face puffy with sleep
above his beard and marked with worry lines.

"You called?" he said.

"We've had a visitor. Karim Faisal," al-Bari told him. "It
appears there has been unrest within the province. Soldiers
killed. The men responsible are still at large."

"How many soldiers?" asked Rashad.

"Twenty, according to Faisal."

"So many, all at once?"

"It is unusual, I know," al-Bari said.

"And what is the significance for us?"

"Unknown. We may trust Brigadier Jadoon as far as his
self-interest grants us power over him, but we must always
be on guard against betrayal. If he feels he can eliminate us
with impunity, then he becomes a danger."

"He can be eliminated," Rashad said. "If other soldiers
have been slain, let those who killed them take the blame for
one more death."

"Not yet. If it is necessary, Arzou Majabein can deal with
him. For now, I prefer to have Jadoon serving us."

"If he does."

"He obeyed our instructions concerning the strike in Islamabad. Jadoon thinks he is working off his debt, but, whether he realizes it or not, each collaboration binds him to al Qaeda more tightly. He is foolish, if he thinks he can escape us."

"Fools exist," Rashad observed. "Some act against their own best interest, especially when frightened."

"I will deal with Brigadier Jadoon," al-Bari said. "Your task is to discover who has chosen this time to begin attacking soldiers in the province. If they prove to be loyal Shiites, counsel them. If they are infidels—or, most particularly, if they seek to harm al Qaeda—they must be stopped."

"Destroyed," Rashad amended.

"But in such a way that we do not reveal ourselves," al-Bari said. "Ideally, we should give them to the army, let the troops avenge their comrades—and be certain that Jadoon acknowledges his debt for our assistance."

"As you say."

"I'm going back to sleep, now," al-Bari said. "It's too early in the morning to be mapping out campaigns."

Without a hint of envy, Rashad said, "Sleep well. I will arrange for all our comrades to be on alert throughout the province. It should not be long before we know the men responsible for the disturbance."

"And remember," al-Bari said, "we must not be tied to their elimination. Nothing should be said or done to make the faithful question our collegiality."

9

U.S. Department of Justice; Washington, D.C.

Hal Brognola's days when he'd been a "brick agent" for the FBI, pounding pavement and building cases that sent felons off to prison for hard time, were long gone. but that was all right. Every man had his place in this war, and his was no longer out in the field.

These days he was needed in Washington, where he was currently fielding terse reports from Pakistan that marked the progress of his long-time friend—a man who, officially, no longer existed.

The reports Brognola had received so far were hardly reassuring. Twenty soldiers killed initially, then twenty-six more—all in Pakistan's North-West Frontier Province by "persons unknown." A full-scale hunt was in progress. Meanwhile yet another suicide bombing had rocked Islamabad.

Brognola racked his brain for possible connections between Bolan's mission and the latter event, but he came up empty. Akram Ben Abd al-Bari might have ordered the bombing, but such things required at least minimal planning. The link just wasn't there.

Brognola wasn't even sure of Bolan's link to the most recent army skirmishes, although they sounded like his style. Hit fast, hit hard, leave no one standing when the smoke cleared. Brognola surmised that the first engagement, coming so soon after Bolan's insertion, was probably coincidental.

As for the second…

Shit happened in the field, as Brognola knew well enough from personal experience. And while Bolan had long ago drawn a personal line that he refused to cross—vowing that he would never kill police, no matter how corrupt or brutal they might be—soldiers did not share that protection.

Hoping there'd be recent news, Brognola placed another call to Stony Man, Kurtzman's direct line. The man picked up on the third ring, with a simple "Yes?"

"Any new word?" Brognola asked without preamble.

"Not since midnight our time," Kurtzman said. "You know we'll keep you updated."

"Sure. I just hoped there might be…something."

"Maybe no news really *is* good news," Kurtzman suggested.

"Right. Keep me post." He disconnected the call.

A few minutes later, Brognola's private line buzzed. He lunged for the receiver, almost fumbling it before he got it to his ear.

"Hello?"

"It's me," a distant voice informed him.

Jack Grimaldi, Bolan's wings.

"Any word?" the pilot asked him.

"Nothing specific, yet," Brognola said. The line was scrambled, but he always played it safe. "We've had two contacts in the field, but nothing traceable. Nothing specific to the job."

He pictured Grimaldi digesting that, not liking it, then heard him say, "Okay. You've got my number there?"

"Got it."

"Okay," the pilot said before the link was severed.

Back to waiting.

Brognola decided he should focus on some other work. He had a presidential briefing scheduled for the day after the next, and a routine audit of his office—the benign, public division of it—by the General Accounting Office.

Meeting with the Man, and with the GAO.

But none of it really mattered, as Brognola pushed the paper piles away from him and longed for one of the cigars he'd given up on doctor's orders.

Waiting for the goddamned telephone to ring.

Jalalabad; Nangarhar Province, Afghanistan

THE CALL to Brognola in Washington had been a waste of time, like everything else Grimaldi had done since Bolan leaped out of his plane over Pakistan.

How long ago had it been? Twenty hours and thirty-nine minutes.

It felt like twenty years.

Grimaldi was accustomed to delivering the Executioner on-target and retrieving him on time, but some missions were worse than others. Most were hit-and-git, with fixed parameters of time and place. Bolan would land at *A* and be picked up at *B* in *X* hours.

It could be nerve-racking, hell yes, but there were limits to the stress.

Not this time.

Grimaldi, as the delivery boy, had not been briefed on any details of the mission beyond where he had to go, and when he had to get there. As for retrieval of his package—Bolan, hopefully alive and in one piece—the time and place was "flexible."

Meaning, nobody had a clue concerning where, when, or if Bolan would exit Pakistan.

Grimaldi flagged the waiter for another coffee—his third, so far—and riffled through his bankroll of Afghanis.

His coffee arrived and Grimaldi paid the waiter before sipping it.

The Stony Man pilot believed in waging the good fight, and he and Bolan had waged more than a few.

They'd logged a couple million miles together, hitting jungles, deserts, urban battlegrounds that rivaled any Third

World war zone, and he always clung to the certainty that Bolan would succeed. That he'd survive.

Each time, that faith was tested, but it hadn't failed.

Not yet.

The café's aging television had been running news for fifteen minutes, but Grimaldi couldn't translate any of the commentary or the Persian text that crawled across the screen like tracks on an electrocardiogram.

Right now, the camera's focus was a pair of burned-out armored vehicles. It looked as if they had been driven down into a desert gully, then torched with some kind of chemical charge. White phosphorous, perhaps, or thermite. Soldiers were picking over the remains, while firefighters stood back and left them to it.

Always something.

Grimaldi had never known a time when people weren't preoccupied with killing one another, and he guessed that no such time would ever come. The question—in his mind, at least—wasn't so much a case of who killed whom, but rather why the killing was performed.

Some predators, human and otherwise, were immune to re-mediation. They wouldn't listen to negotiations, felt no empathy. They were, in fact, devoid of any feeling beyond an insatiable hunger.

Bolan was strong, smart and slick enough to handle them, provided he wasn't overwhelmed by numbers or betrayed by one he trusted. The problem with stalking predators, simply stated, was that they never died out.

It was a predatory world out there, and those who swam against the tide, resisting it, were always outnumbered. Always outgunned.

This time, Grimaldi knew, Bolan was not only tracking al Qaeda's elite, but he was doing it while trying to avoid God only knew how many soldiers, whose commanders might share ideologies with Bolan's targets. Might even be guarding them, either to keep the peace at home or to support al Qaeda's terrorist attacks abroad.

Just give me the coordinates, Grimaldi thought, and let me take the bastards out.

But it was not to be.

He drained his coffee and stepped from the café into another scorching day.

Sunshine, blue skies and death.

The perfect package, right.

"HOW MUCH FARTHER?" Bolan asked Gorshani.

"Half an hour, perhaps," his driver said. "These are the Safed Koh, ahead of us."

Daylight was just an hour old, already casting shadows on the rugged range of peaks that lay across their path like a natural roadblock. Bolan knew the two-lane highway would take them through those mountains and beyond, but his trek ended somewhere in their midst.

He didn't ask which one was Mount Khakwani, didn't care at that point. There'd be time enough to size it up once they had reached the mountain's base and were prepared to start their climb. Until then, the Executioner used his time to watch out for patrols, coming or going.

Someone had found the burned-out APCs sooner than Bolan had hoped they would. A news broadcast from Radio Buraq Peshawar, translated by Gorshani while it played, had given sketchy details of "ruthless massacre," with vows from persons in authority that those responsible would be tracked down and punished.

No surprise, there, but it meant their time was running short.

The net would already be cast, and if they met a search team on its way to Mount Khakwani, it would mean another critical delay at best.

Assuming they survived a third skirmish.

Bolan believed in luck to some extent, though he had

always been convinced that people made much of their own through preparation, courage and commitment to whatever cause they served. If they were lazy, negligent and weak, it stood to reason that their luck would normally be bad.

But, on the other hand, no training, no amount of guts would stop a well-aimed shot from mangling flesh and bone. No soldier was invincible, whether he dressed from head to toe in Kevlar or was buttoned down inside an APC. For each defense, there was a weapon built to pierce and overcome it.

Bolan had been putting off a question that he had to ask Gorshani, but he voiced it now. "Somebody must have briefed you on coordinates for where we're going," he remarked. "I need to know your contact's name before we hit the slopes."

Gorshani shot a glance at him, surprised, then turned back toward the road. "But I was told—"

"To keep me in the dark," Bolan said, interrupting. "I get that, and it's no good. If you think we've had trouble up to now, forget about it. Once we're on the mountain, *that's* when it starts getting hairy. If it goes south on us, but we make it out alive somehow, there'll be a need for payback on the setup. I'll be reaching out to touch someone."

"Goes south? Payback?" This time, Gorshani sounded nervous *and* confused.

"A name," Bolan replied. "Right now."

Finally, reluctantly, Gorshani said, "Azar Gulpari. He contacted me through…others."

"Your controller from the Agency," Bolan surmised.

Gorshani nodded.

"Okay. Who is Azar Gulpari?"

"As I understand it, he has been a member of al Qaeda since the group was organized. Over the years, his allegiance to bin Laden and the rest has apparently weakened, but he cannot simply leave. To leave is death, you understand?"

"Blood in, blood out," Bolan replied.

"Sorry?"

"It's an expression used by criminals back in the States. It means you spill blood when you join the gang, to prove yourself, and they spill yours if you try getting out."

Gorshani nodded. "It is the same, I think. And since he cannot leave the group, Gulpari hopes to bring it down. It think it is perhaps his one hope to cleanse his conscience."

"And he told you all this?" Bolan made no attempt to hide his skepticism.

"No. Most of it was explained to me by my controller, as you say. Gulpari told me only what I—what we—need to know in order to find al-Bari and the rest."

"So, what was your impression of him? Was he straight with you? Did anything ring hollow?"

"I am here," Gorshani said simply. "If I believed that he was lying, that the story was a means to take my life, I would not have been waiting when you dropped out of the sky."

That much, at least, Bolan believed. And it was all the he would get until they took their shot at Mount Khakwani.

"Right, then," Bolan said. "Let's get it done."

ARZOU MAJABEIN hated bearing bad news. Even mixed with good news, as his was, the bad reflected on its bearer. It could sometimes be a death sentence for those with no actual responsibility for what had gone awry.

Majabein's face was stoic as he confronted the guards outside Akram Ben Abd al-Bari's cave. He offered no objection as they frisked him, then ran metal-detecting wands over his body from turban to toes.

He had, as usual, left all his weapons in his car.

When he was cleared for passage, Majabein followed his silent escort into the familiar darkness of the cavern, listened to the crunching echo of their footsteps as they left daylight behind. Beyond the first turn in the tunnel, more guards waited. Majabein was handed off to them, his guide retreating toward his post outside.

Another frisk, no wands this time, and then he stood before his masters, with al-Bari seated in the middle of a stony dais, with Ra'id Ibn Rashad at his right hand. Majabein hoped that neither man could see him trembling as he stepped forward, knelt and bowed his head.

"You bring word from Islamabad," al-Bari said.

"I do, sir. And other news, besides."

"Begin."

"The martyr's sacrifice was flawless. Nineteen infidels were slain outright, with twenty-three more wounded. Some of those will die, I am convinced. Also, the damage to their property is costly and significant."

"What was the martyr's name?" Rashad inquired.

"Sabeir Hamayun, an Afghani. Pamphlets with his photo are in circulation now. Al Jazeera plans to air the standard profile on him, probably tomorrow or the next day."

"There were no objections from the brigadier?" al-Bari asked.

"No, sir. Bahaar Jadoon is in our debt for life. He played his part exactly as directed."

"Very well. You mentioned other news?"

"Yes, sir." Majabein cleared his throat and moved on to the bad. "Last night—or, I should say, early this morning— someone ambushed an army patrol to the south, at a village called Sanjrani. According to the news reports, and confirmed by our contacts inside the FIA, twenty-six soldiers were killed. Also, nine villagers. The highest-ranking officer was a colonel, Salim Laghari, who served as an aide to our own brigadier."

Al-Bari and Rashad exchanged somber glances, before al-Bari said, "These dead soldiers you speak of, are they not the same reported to us earlier last night?"

Majabein risked a shrug. "Sir, I don't know who spoke to you, or what was said. The skirmish I describe was fought sometime after midnight, this morning. I am aware of another ambush, still farther south, that killed twenty soldiers yesterday afternoon."

"Two attacks, then," Rashad said, confirming it.

"Yes, sir."

"I take it," al-Bari said, "that this colonel from Rawalpindi was dispatched to find the killers from the first attack?"

"It seems so, sir," Majabein said.

"Sent by our brigadier."

"Most likely, yes, sir."

"Two attacks, still unexplained. The second farther north…and so, closer to us."

"Yes, sir."

Al-Bari did not ask if they were in danger. He had to know that every move he made and every breath he drew was fraught with risk. Al Qaeda's top commanders had lived on borrowed time since the 9/11 attacks, and while some seemed almost forgotten in the West, Majabein knew that al-Bari and Rashad were too wily to take their survival for granted.

"I think the brigadier might benefit from certain reassurances," al-Bari said. "You will inform him, if he harbors any doubts, that we had no part in the slaying of his men. We have no quarrel with the Pakistani people or their government, only with infidels whose heresy pollutes the Islamic republic."

"It shall be done, sir."

"And tell him, also, that if he requires assistance in pursuing those who slew his soldiers, he may call on us at any time. We have resources that may not be readily available to politicians or to men in uniform."

"Yes, sir."

Al-Bari did not have to add that if Jadoon requested help from agents of al Qaeda, he would thus increase his debt of service. It was a masterstroke, designed at once to seal a pact of friendship and to turn the screws, commanding strict obedience from one who might, someday, discover that he could not serve two masters simultaneously.

"Make haste," al-Bari said, "before our friend does something rash, even irreparable."

Majabein bowed his way out of the cave and jogged past the guards to his car. A long drive lay before him, back to Peshawar, and there would be no time for rest along the way. Failing in this assignment would erase whatever praise he had received for other work, and might cost Majabein his life.

He gunned the old car's engine, aimed it down the mountain and was off.

"WE SHOULD CONSIDER leaving this place," Ra'id Ibn Rashad said.

"I have considered it," al-Bari told his friend and colleague. "First, we need another place to go."

"The world is full of caves," Rashad answered.

Was there a hint of bitterness behind his words?

"You wish to be a public figure once again?" al-Bari asked. "To have reporters on your doorstep?"

"No, Akram. I never had your talent as a speaker, and besides, the war of words was lost in 1948. Armed struggle is the only answer for our people and our faith. I understand the need for sacrifice, but I won't lie and say that I enjoy living in burrows, with the lizards and scorpions."

"You still miss Ara and Fareiba," al-Bari said.

"Yes. Of course."

Rashad's wife and daughter had been killed by agents of Mossad, six years before, during a bungled effort to assassinate Rashad himself. Only al-Bari knew how much his friend had grieved—and how he had avenged himself by sending Semtex-laden martyrs into Tel Aviv, Jerusalem and Haifa for the next twelve months, claiming a hundred lives for each of those he'd lost.

But it would never be enough.

"They wait for you in Paradise," al-Bari said.

"Perhaps they wait in vain," Rashad answered.

Al-Bari's frown demanded explanation. With a weary sigh, Rashad said, "I am dedicated to our struggle. This, you know.

It has consumed my family and will consume my life, someday. As for the rest... Akram, sometimes I doubt that I am worthy of a place in Paradise with Ara and Fareiba, with the others we have lost."

"Allah rewards his faithful soldiers," al-Bari said.

"He also reads our hearts," Rashad answered. "In reading mine, he may discover that my hatred of the enemy has left no room for love of him."

"Do not profane your lips with heresy."

"I speak only the truth, old friend. But never fear that I will leave your side. Where else would I be welcome, after all?"

Uneasy with the new direction of their conversation, al-Bari changed the subject. "We must tighten our security precautions," he observed. "More guards, to start with. And if Arzou Majabein remains unsatisfied after his meeting with the brigadier, then we can move."

"As you think best," Rashad replied.

"You need more rest," al-Bari told him.

"All I do is rest, and think. I would not mind some action, for a change."

Al-Bari smiled at that. "We're not foot soldiers anymore, my friend. That part of life has passed us by. We're generals, now."

"Meaning, we have the will to fight, but not the strength." Rashad's face wore a rueful smile.

"Faith *is* our strength," al-Bari said. "And hatred of the enemies who would destroy that faith."

"You're right, of course, Akram."

"I will instruct Fahim to reinforce the guard. Perhaps two dozen men, rotating shifts?"

Rashad nodded. "Beyond that, we'll be overcrowded, like an anthill. Don't forget additional supplies."

"And we must plan a new campaign abroad," al-Bari said. "America, I think, but not the Eastern Seaboard. A target that exemplifies the decadence and the hypocrisy of the Crusaders."

"Why not Hollywood?" Rashad inquired. "It's owned and run by Zionists, corrupting all the world."

"Or possibly Las Vegas," al-Bari said, "where the Christians flock to throw their cash away."

"More Zionists," Rashad observed. "They built and own the great casinos. Half their money goes to Israel, and the rest to whores."

"To whores and politicians," al-Bari said.

"What's the difference?" Rashad asked.

Al-Bari smiled at that, regretting that he had forgotten how to laugh. His faith, his war, had cost him mirth, on top of all the rest that he had lost.

"Perhaps none," he acknowledged. "Allah hates them all."

"His will be done," Rashad said.

10

Gorshani drove his SUV off-road, along a dry creek bed, which, Bolan guessed, would fill with rushing water during flash-flood season. That was weeks away, however, and his mission on the mountain should be finished, one way or the other, before dawn the following day.

When they'd driven a half mile or so into the gully, and its steep, unstable walls of dirt were four feet taller than the SUV, Gorshani stopped, switched off the engine and declared, "We hide it here."

Ahead of them, Bolan observed the gully clogged with Russian thistle, known in the United States as tumbleweeds. Nodding, he pulled his gear out of the vehicle, set it aside and donned his gloves, then helped Gorshani camouflage the dusty SUV. The clumps of thorny, dried-out vegetation would mask it from an aerial perspective, and from casual inspection at ground level.

Doing the job properly took twenty minutes. It left Bolan sweating, but he knew that he'd be cool again once they had reached a higher elevation. Mount Khakwani towered over them, roughly eleven thousand feet in height, but seeming taller from their mole's-eye view.

Somewhere close to the summit, Bolan hoped to find Akram Ben Abd al-Bari and a handful of his closest aides. The more, the merrier, in fact—up to a point.

As they divided up the climbing gear, Bolan wondered whether his guide would make it to the top—or wherever al-

Bari might be waiting for them. Gorshani had proved he could fight and kill, in the crunch, but aiming and pulling a trigger required no great strength of endurance. It was the difference between a fifty-yard dash and a marathon.

Bolan's early Special Forces training had included mountaineering, and he'd kept himself in fighting form since then. Still, based on what Gorshani had told him so far, he understood most of their climb would rank as tough hiking, rather than scaling vertical cliffs or scrabbling over glaciers.

The ropes, carabiners and pitons were gear they *might* need, but which, with any luck, would not be used. However it might pan out, the extra weight was worth it, for the peace of mind that it provided.

Their first step toward the mountain—their final destination—was evacuation of the gully where they had concealed Gorshani's SUV. They walked back almost to where they had left the highway, then climbed up the crumbling bank to ground level. From there, they jogged the final hundred feet to reach the base of Mount Khakwani.

Up close and personal, Bolan saw there was no shortage of trails. He scanned the mountainside, saw one that seemed to go the farthest up without visible interruption, and confirmed the choice with Gorshani. A nod from his guide, and they started to climb.

The slope began at thirty-odd degrees and steepened after that, lighting a fire in Bolan's thigh and calf muscles, testing his stamina before he'd covered forty yards. His gear seemed to gain weight with every stride, and while Gorshani carried less, Bolan could hear his labored breathing up ahead.

Beyond the physical exertion, Bolan had to deal with the fact that they were completely exposed to any trackers on the ground or sentries posted higher on the mountain. Like a pair of insects crawling up a kitchen wall, they could be swatted down at any time. Bolan's fatigues gave him some cover, but the desert camo pattern didn't blend as well with shale and granite, as with sand and gravel. Still, he guessed that he was no worse off than his companion, clad in a brown jacket and a pair of denim jeans.

We're in it now, he thought. Too late to second-guess the wardrobe.

If they were observed, they would be killed, regardless of their clothing choices. Bolan's mission had been a gamble from the moment he'd accepted it. And now he moved into the finals where the stakes were life or death.

What else is new? he asked himself, and settled into the long haul.

LIEUTENANT COLONEL Raheem Davi stood above the burned-out hulks of two M113 armored personnel carriers, breathing in the still-strong smells of burned gasoline, electrical wiring and flesh. The bodies had been carted off before he'd gotten there, but their essence had remained behind, part of the desert atmosphere.

It troubled Davi to think that each time he smelled something—be it a flower, a succulent steak, or a pile of feces—he was, in fact, inhaling microscopic pieces of the thing itself. Each smell on Earth had substance, and that knowledge, once acquired, had made him almost paranoid about the effluent his brain and body might absorb simply by breathing.

Still, he had to be here, and his soldiers would have ridiculed him if he'd worn a surgical mask to the scene of the crime. Weakness was punished in the military, one way or another, even more than in the world at large.

So he inhaled the stench of death and tried to relish it, become one with his men, who didn't flinch as they perused the battleground.

Davi's assignment was simplicity itself, at least on paper. He would find the men responsible for this atrocity, as well as the annihilation of a previous patrol, and either kill them or take them back to Peshawar for judgment. That had been

Colonel Salim Laghari's assignment, but he had failed spec-
tacularly, thereby giving Davi his one chance to shine.

Where would the killers go from here? he asked himself.

There first ambush of troops had occurred some eighty
miles to the south of the killing ground where Davi now
stood, proof positive that they were moving northward—if,
in fact, the same men were responsible for both events. Davi
assumed that they must be, since tracking down two different guerrilla bands within the time allotted to him clearly was
impossible.

The brigadier had given Davi just twelve hours to produce
results, by any means required. Once that deadline ran out,
he was at risk of being sidelined and relieved of duty, suffering disgrace that might prove fatal to his career. Success,
conversely, would ensure his status as a rising star.

"There was an extra corpse," Davi remarked.

"Yes, sir," Company Havildar Major Minhas Kermani
replied.

"Twenty-seven," Davi said. "There should be only twenty-
six."

"You are correct, sir."

"So, they had a prisoner?"

"Most likely, sir," Kermani said.

"What is the nearest village?" Davi asked.

"Sanjrani, I believe, sir. It lies five miles to the south."

"We'll start there," Davi said, "and see if anyone is
missing. If they are, then someone else will know why they
were taken, and we work from there."

"Yes, sir."

Five minutes later they were rolling southward on the
narrow rural highway, buttoned down inside the APCs as if
expecting an attack at any moment. Which, in fact, Lieutenant Colonel Davi was.

He planned to crack the mystery that had been handed to
him, not wind up as one more name on a growing death list.

He would not make the brigadier regret selecting him for this assignment, or bring shame upon his brigade.

There was no substitute for victory.

The APCs reached Sanjrani fifteen minutes after departing the massacre scene—or, rather, the point where the victims were left. It was apparent from the scene they'd left behind that the soldiers and their unknown passenger had been slain somewhere else, then transported to the gully where they had been found.

Sanjrani was as good a place as any to start looking.

At the village, Davi summoned the peasants from their homes with his APC's PA system, and waited impatiently as they straggled into a rough crowd formation before him. His call for the headman caused another brief delay, before a thin old man stepped forward.

"What is your name?" Davi demanded.

"Armin Mojtaba, sir," the old man said.

"What happened to your face?"

Mojtaba raised a hand to feel his nose and lips, as if the bruising and scabbed-over cut were new to him, instead of hours old.

"A disagreement, sir. It has been settled."

"Ah. A disagreement over what? With whom?"

"Sir, it was trivial."

"Your injuries do not appear so."

"It is best forgotten now, sir."

Even Davi's men were startled when he drew his sidearm, pressed its muzzle to Mojtaba's wrinkled forehead and drew back the hammer with his thumb.

"Old man," Davi said, "my brigade has lost twenty-six men. Another twenty were assassinated yesterday. I think you know what happened to them, and the matter is not trivial to me."

"Sir, with respect, you are mistaken."

"I can live with that mistake," Davi informed him. "You cannot."

A solitary tear spilled down the old man's weathered
face, then he began to speak.

THE NEW GUARDS were mostly Taliban, black-turbaned, with
their beards untended. They seemed to have the proper
attitude, which meant they had forgotten how to smile and
likely would have died before they laughed at anything, even
the downfall of America.

It made for peace and quiet in the cave complex that Akram
Ben Abd al-Bari called home. Without a noisy staff, he could
devote himself entirely to the vital tasks of planning and spiri-
tual meditation. In al-Bari's mind, there was no concrete difference between the two.

Jihad, as he had known and served it all his life, meant
struggling or striving in the way of Allah. It involved an endless
war against the heathen West and its puppet state of Israel.

To each his own. So be it.

At the moment, he was more concerned with fatwa than
jihad. The former, generally, was an edict on Islamic law and
could be issued by any Muslim scholar. In modern, practical
terms, fatwa was understood to be a death sentence, issued
upon an infidel or blasphemer.

Ironically, throughout the Muslim world there was unani-
mous agreement that a fatwa only bound its author. Thus
judicial chaos was averted, and a semblance of sanity preserved. However, when al-Bari pronounced a fatwa, he had
the soldiers and resources of al Qaeda to carry out his orders.

Al-Bari wished to kill the unknown men responsible for
stirring up the hornet's nest of military action in the province,
but he could not send a squad to liquidate them if he didn't
know their names, or where they might be found.

Rashad had hinted that the killings might have something
to do with al-Bari himself, or their mountain retreat. It seemed
implausible, and yet...

When he plotted the two mass killings on a map, it did

seem that the killers had to be moving north, along a route that would bring them into the Safed Koh. That did not mean they would wind up on Mount Khakwani, but if there was any possibility of it, al-Bari had to be prepared.

He hated running from the enemy, although strategic withdrawals were a guerrilla's stock-in-trade. He longed to stand and fight—to test himself again, as he had in his youth—but al-Bari knew he had to consider first the broad needs of al Qaeda and those who dedicated everything they had to his jihad.

His spies were scouring the countryside for any lead as to who'd killed the soldiers, watching the approaches to al-Bari's lair. If he was found...

The prospect almost made him smile. Surely, if the Crusaders knew where to find him, they would have sent cruise missiles to destroy al-Bari long ago. Long-distance killing was their specialty, followed by boasting to the media.

But if not the Crusaders, then, who?

Al-Bari knew that he had to also watch his friends, while taking bold steps to eradicate his enemies. Unfortunately, when he did not know the men who possibly were bent on killing him, he had to guard against all men in general.

And women, too, although females had played no significant part in his life since the massacre of his wife and daughters. It has been said that "no man is an island," but al-Bari considered himself a mountain.

He was a rugged mountain—or, at least, a part of one— and that was where he felt best able to defend himself. Anyone who sought him there had to run a gauntlet of his own devising, and face death before he found al-Bari.

In the meantime, while he waited to see if Rashad's suggestions were prophecy or paranoia, al-Bari had a war to run. There would be fresh blood on his hands by this time the next day.

It would be, he hoped, his ticket into Paradise.

GORSHANI WAS starting to drag, and they weren't even halfway to the summit yet. Bolan sympathized with his guide, guessing that Gorshani hadn't kept himself in shape for this kind of exertion, but the Executioner couldn't let the pace slack off.

To help distract Gorshani from his weariness, the burning ache that made his legs feel leaden, Bolan questioned him about al Qaeda's operations in the province and in Pakistan at large.

"I take it that the military doesn't interfere," he said.

"Rarely," Gorshani answered, almost gasping. "If a terrorist parades himself too openly, he risks arrest. But otherwise…"

"You mean, 'Don't ask, don't tell'?"

"Yes. Exactly."

"And do you have some extremists inside the military itself?"

"Almost assuredly."

That would explain the government's persistent inability to trace fugitive terrorist leaders "hiding" in Pakistan, or to arrest the men behind domestic suicide bombings.

"How extensive do you think the infiltration is?" Bolan asked.

On the trail in front of him, Gorshani paused to catch his breath, then labored onward, answering over his shoulder.

"When I was in the army, we were never told to help al Qaeda or the other groups. Nor were we sent to rub them out. And I never heard discussion of them in the barracks, unless there had been a bombing."

"Someone must determine policy," Bolan replied. "There's always one man at the top, or close to it, who calls the tune."

After another twenty yards, Gorshani said, "Perhaps…it may be…Brigadier Jadoon."

"Who's that?" Bolan asked, picking up his pace to ride on Gorshani's heels.

"His name is mentioned in the newspapers, sometimes on television, when there is a bombing or a skirmish with the rebels. His brigade, I think, is meant to deal with such things."

"And how's he doing?"

Bolan's guide found strength enough to shrug.

"He is not criticized, of course. I think where common bandits are concerned, he is effective."

"And with terrorists?"

"Again, it would depend on who they are. Those who attack the government, of course, are doomed. But if they only strike at Jews or infidels, they are unlikely to be charged."

"And this Jadoon works out of Rawalpindi?"

"I assume so. Army headquarters is there."

Something to think about, before he left the country. Bolan wasn't sure that taking out the man in charge of giving terrorists a free pass would have any lasting impact on state policy, but it was worth a try.

"The trail is narrowing," Gorshani said.

Bolan had seen it coming, but he wasn't worried yet. At least there was a trail. They weren't dangling from ropes, like spiders on a strand of silk, with no options for movement if their adversaries spotted them.

Which adversaries?

Down below, he knew more soldiers would be hunting them. Whether they traced the APCs back to Sanjrani and got information there, or worked out that the trail was leading north and they then scoured the countryside in that direction, Bolan recognized the risk of being overtaken by more Pakistani regulars or paramilitary troops. A battle on the mountainside, especially if they committed aircraft to the hunt, would likely be a losing proposition.

On the other hand, there was no doubt that when they reached al-Bari's hideout, they would find it guarded by the toughest gunmen that al Qaeda could recruit. Bolan expected nothing less than absolute resistance to the death, and he was willing to accommodate all comers.

But he needed the advantage of surprise.

So, as the rugged mountain trail grew steeper, he dug in and did everything within his power to ignore the protests from his aching muscles. If and when they had to use the ropes and pitons, the Executioner would grit his teeth and do the job he'd been assigned without complaint.

A spider's nest was waiting for him near the peak of Mount Khakwani, and he meant to clean it out, once and for all. From there, well, he would have to wait and see what happened next.

But he would keep the Pakistani brigadier in mind.

And, given half a chance, he'd teach the friend of terrorists what it was like to live in a terror of his own.

11

Lieutenant Colonel Raheem Davi left the village of Sanjrani with the information he required. He also left behind a broken headman and the corpses of two younger peasants who had tried to interrupt Davi's interrogation of Armin Mojtaba.

He had finished off the dead men personally, after they were wounded by his soldiers. Davi felt that it was necessary to establish a rapport between himself and those who served him, and to build his reputation as an officer who stopped at nothing to achieve his goals.

Sanjrani's villagers would fear him now, and if that fear was tinged with hatred, what of it? More to the point, Davi's own men would know that he was not afraid to soil his hands, and that he would not try to blame them for the killings later, if an inquest was convened.

But there would be no inquest—Davi was sure of that. The information he'd obtained from Mojtaba identified one of the men responsible for wiping out Colonel Salim Laghari's unit—and, most likely, slaughtering Second Lieutenant Tarik Naseer's patrol the previous day.

Hussein Gorshani.

It was not a name that Davi would forget. He had already radioed the news to Peshawar, and had contacted Brigadier Jadoon in Rawalpindi. Davi did not plan to let an intermediary give Jadoon the traitor's name, and possibly claim credit for securing it. Careers were built in such ways, and if anyone advanced for this day's work, Davi meant for that person to be him.

No one in Sanjrani had been able to identify Gorshani's traveling companion, but they had agreed that he was *ajnabi,* a foreigner. Beyond that, they could only say that he was a white man, but the fine point of his nationality had eluded them.

American or British?

Davi understood that the Americans were the prime movers in the so-called war on terror. London usually followed any course laid out by Washington, to preserve their special relationship, but British soldiers were unlikely to come hunting with a Pakistan traitor in the North-West Frontier Province.

As to who they hunted, Davi had a fairly good idea. He knew that refugees from the American invasion of Afghanistan were sheltered in his country, many of them right here in this very province. He assumed that some of them were criminals, in Western terms, though Shiite fundamentalists might disagree.

The killers Davi sought were hunting agents of al Qaeda—and not just any agents. No American would risk his life in Pakistan to kill a bomb maker or some midlevel officer. They were, Davi had been informed, making their way toward Mount Khakwani, where rumor had it some of the top men in al Qaeda might be found.

Not *the* top man, of course.

His hideout would be known to only half a dozen people in the world, none of them wearing Pakistani uniforms. He, who had fired the first great salvos at America nearly a decade earlier, would not trust any government official with the knowledge of his whereabouts at any given time. The price placed on his head—in dollars, and in other equally valuable currency—was far too large and tempting for the common man or woman to resist.

But there were others, Davi knew, a step or two below the top man, who were slightly more accessible. And if they could be found, they could be killed.

And should Davi attempt to stop it?

His primary goal, of course, had to be to find and punish those responsible for killing more than forty of his fellow officers and soldiers in a single day. Already, based on information he'd provided, agents of the FIA and ISI would be dissecting Hussein Gorshani's life, poring over any dossiers they might possess, or starting files, if none existed. Soon, they would know every member of his family, alive or dead, and those still living would regret their family ties to an enemy of the state.

As for Gorshani's still unnamed companion, the foreigner, there was nowhere to begin searching for his identity. Only when Davi had the stranger in his grasp, or lying dead before him, could the task of learning who he was and who he represented finally begin.

So, they were bound for Mount Khakwani, in pursuit of two known terrorists and murderers. Davi hadn't asked for permission to pursue them. It was part of his assignment, or at the very least implicit in the orders he'd received from Brigadier Bahaar Jadoon.

Locate the killers. Capture or destroy them.

Simple.

Davi could decide about the other targets—what to do with them, and how it would affect his prospects for promotion—if and when his quarry led him to their mountain sanctuary.

In the meantime, he would focus simply on the kill.

THE TRAIL HAD TURNED into a narrow track that mountain goats might find convenient, but every step that Bolan took reminded him that it was only six or seven inches wider than the waffle soles of his rough-out combat boots.

Plenty of room for walking—as long as you placed one

foot directly in front of the other and avoided any sideslippage as if your life depended on it.

Which it did.

They had covered roughly half the ground required to reach their final target, and a stumble here meant plummeting three thousand feet—and the remains among the rocks and trees below would be unrecognizable as human, but for the shreds of clothing and twisted, shattered gear.

Bolan was not afraid of heights, but there was no point looking down into the vast chasm below him. Rather, he preferred to focus on Gorshani, still leading, although the altitude and angle of the grade had slowed his pace.

The narrow ledge offered no place for them to rest.

The simple act of crouching would be perilous, particularly with the gear that Bolan carried. Gusts of mountain wind already threatened to propel them from their perch. Bolan guessed that they would likely find a resting place somewhere above, before the trail ended.

If he was wrong on that score, they would just keep climbing through the bone-numbing fatigue and be prepared to fight when they arrived.

If they arrived.

Each passing moment made pursuit more likely for the killings at Sanjrani, and the ones before it. How long would it be before some officer or agent managed to identify Gorshani? Bolan would have bet that certain people in the village knew where he was going with Gorshani, even if they had no grasp of why.

But motive didn't matter, if the enemy could track his movements. It would then turn into a horse race. Perhaps it already had.

"We need to speed this up," he told Gorshani.

"I will try."

"You know what happens if they catch us out here, in the open."

"Yes."

"Dig down and show me something."

With a gasp that might've been a sob, Gorshani found some small reserve of strength inside himself and struck a faster pace. They weren't exactly double-timing—which, in any case, would probably have sent them plunging into space within a hundred yards—but they were doing better. Making better time.

Small favors, Bolan thought, and matched his weary guide's pace step for step.

He had considered leaving Gorshani at the base of the mountain. The guide part of Gorshani's job was basically over once they'd started up the one and only alternative track to Mount Khakwani's summit. Bolan doubted he'd need a translator when he arrived.

He didn't plan on questioning Akram Ben Abd al-Bari or the others, when they met, much less suggesting any deals. His mission was straightforward search and destroy, with no option for discussion or surrender. Anything al-Bari or his cronies had to say could be said with their guns.

And Bolan would reply in kind.

In fact, if all went well and Bolan saw them first, they'd have no time to work out who was killing them.

So, yes, a case could be made that he should've left Gorshani with the SUV, but when he'd floated the suggestion, Bolan's driver had appeared to feel insulted.

In the crunch, Gorshani argued that he'd proved himself in battle, and that Bolan would be foolish to reject an extra pair of hands—an extra gun—when he was facing lethal odds.

He was correct on both points, and there'd been nothing to gain by cutting him from the team. Now, even though Bolan might wish Gorshani was behind him on the narrow sloping trail, he knew the Pakistani would be helpful once they reached their target.

They were going in with no intelligence beyond the

general location of al-Bari's cave and the belief that he would be in residence. They didn't know how many shooters would be ranged against them, or if there'd be booby traps planted along the way.

It was a live-and-learn experience.

Bolan could only hope that it would not be learn and die.

BRIGADIER BAHAAR Jadoon knew that he should be pleased to have learned the name of one of the men responsible for so much of his trouble in the past twenty-four hours, but he could not find the strength to smile.

He had, of course, congratulated Raheem Davi on discovering the name and filed that mental credit slip away for future reference. There would be no preventing Davi's elevation to full colonel now, unless he bungled the remainder of his task so badly that the blame would be attached to him alone.

Or, if by chance, he did not make it back alive.

Jadoon knew where his enemies were going, now. Davi might overtake them on the road, but it seemed doubtful, with the lead that they had to have. In fact, they should have already reached the mountain, and perhaps be scaling it by one means or another, to complete what he assumed to be their task.

The question now was should Brigadier Jadoon attempt to stop them?

Davi, obviously, would pursue the killers with his flying squad of troops, but these men had already annihilated two patrols of equal size. There was a real chance that Lieutenant Colonel Davi might, himself, meet with the same fate as Salim Laghari and the others who had preceded him.

And what of it?

Jadoon bore no animosity toward Davi, nor did he treasure him. Junior officers were perfectly expendable. Risk came with delegation of responsibility.

Why else did they exist?

Jadoon's thoughts focused, rather, on the danger to Akram Ben Abd al-Bari and his circle of subordinates. If they were killed by traitors, or by someone from outside Pakistan, how would it harm or profit *him?*

Officially, al-Bari and the other leaders of al Qaeda were not acknowledged as existing anywhere inside the country. Thus, their liquidation might be buried as a nonevent, unless it was reported to the world at large.

Would the Americans or Brits crow over such a victory?

Perhaps. But without proof…

Deniability was critical. There had to be, at all cost, no photographs, videotapes, or any other concrete record of al-Bari's life or death in Pakistan. His execution, if it was the will of Allah, could not be established as a fact.

That meant preventing the assassins from escaping, after they had done the deed, and confiscating—no, destroying—any evidence collected in the process.

As for al Qaeda itself, Jadoon thought that he might be better off if this Gorshani person and his unknown friend succeeded in their quest to kill al-Bari, Rashad and the rest of them. How better to lift the curse that had haunted Jadoon and colored all parts of his life, both professional and private? His debts to al Qaeda would die with al-Bari, leaving Jadoon free at last.

He could not ask Davi to delay pursuit of the assassins, naturally. That would light a new fuse of suspicion leading back to Brigadier Jadoon himself. But he could pray with new, unrivaled fervor that Allah would lead Davi astray, just long enough to let Gorshani and the foreigner achieve their goal.

At which point, they had to be destroyed without having an opportunity to speak.

It was for spies and politicians to determine who had sent the killers, to debate it endlessly, then finally ignore it or accuse someone in print, perhaps before the General Assembly of the United Nations. Jadoon doubted that it would come to that, but it did not concern him, either way.

His mission was to stop the killers…just as long as he did not stop them too soon.

His phone rang, and Jadoon answered with weary resignation. It would likely be someone of higher rank, calling to harass him with questions and suggestions, or some new report about Gorshani's family, his background, his—

"We need to meet," Majabein said.

Mouthing a silent curse, Jadoon—aware of the possibility that his words were being overheard—said, "I'm afraid that won't be possible, just now. I'm in the midst of something critical."

"And perhaps I can assist you," Majabein replied.

"Perhaps?"

"Nothing in life is guaranteed, but death."

"I cannot spare much time."

"I don't require much time," Majabein said. "Simply a message…for your ears, alone."

Jadoon resigned himself to one more meeting with the little ferret. Allah willing, it would be their last.

"The same place, then?" he asked.

"In half an hour," Majabein replied, and broke the link.

That didn't leave Jadoon much time, but it should be enough. Locking his office door, he told his orderly that he would be available by cell phone for the next hour or so, and then would be returning to his office. Waiting for the elevator, Jadoon checked the pistol tucked inside his belt, beneath his uniform jacket, and felt for the spring-loaded knife in his pocket.

As ready now as he would ever be, Bahaar Jadoon prepared to face his final summons from al Qaeda.

RAWALPINDI'S LARGEST marketplace was thronged with shoppers at midday. Police moved through the crush in pairs, but Arzou Majabein knew they were merely watching out for thieves, pickpockets and the like. If someone had been hunting him, it would be soldiers dressed in olive drab, not khaki shirts and polished badges, whistles draped around their necks.

It had been risky, calling Brigadier Jadoon at headquarters in the midst of a full-scale manhunt, but what choice did he have? Al-Bari had commanded it, and disobedience meant death.

He wondered if the old men were afraid, sitting inside their dreary cave while strangers slaughtered forty, fifty Pakistani troops to reach them. All to kill them.

After being hunted for a decade, living with the threat of sudden death on an hourly basis, did fear still exist? Might the end, when it came and released them to Allah, not be a relief?

Majabein could only answer for himself, with an emphatic negative, but it was not the same. His name *was* found on certain Wanted lists throughout the West and Middle East, but he had never been notorious enough to merit a six-figure bounty or life underground.

Mobility was his blessing.

But it could also be a curse.

If the unknown enemies reached al-Bari and Rashad, then Majabein would be cut adrift. He had no means of reaching the top man to ask for guidance, sanctuary, anything at all. He could, of course, put out the word through trusted contacts, but in times like these, if trust was misplaced...

Majabein shrugged off the morbid turn of thought, focusing briefly on the knives displayed at one market stall. Edged weapons fascinated him, but when the odds were stacked against him, he would take an AK-47 any day.

At last, with only three minutes remaining to their deadline, Majabein saw Brigadier Jadoon approaching. He was still in uniform, no effort to disguise himself, but most of those he passed made a determined effort *not* to notice him. Staring at soldiers—more particularly, those of an exalted rank—might be construed as an offense, regardless of the ogler's intent.

"Peace of God be with you," Majabein said, in greeting.

Jadoon replied with a perfunctory "As it shall be with you," and kept on walking, forcing Majabein to follow and keep pace with him.

"How can you help me?" the brigadier asked.

"First," Majabein replied, "I am instructed to advise you that our master and al Qaeda had no part in the recent killing of your men."

"They weren't all my men," Jadoon told him. "Only some."

"In any case, there is no question of al Qaeda having any hand in those events."

"I never thought you did," Jadoon replied. "Al-Bari isn't fool enough to bite the hand that feeds him."

Majabein slanted a glance toward Jadoon, seeking some evidence of levity. The brigadier's remark verged on insulting. Did it call for a response?

Jadoon's voice interrupted Majabein's consideration of the problem.

"What about that help?" he asked again.

"We have resources, as you know," Majabein said.

"Yes, yes. Go on."

"All of our eyes within the North-West Frontier Province seek the men whom you are hunting. If we find them—"

"What? You'll call me? Kill them for me? *What?*"

The flare of temper startled Majabein. In all their prior dealings, Brigadier Jadoon had been polite and deferential, as befit a man whose life and fortune lay within al-Bari's hands.

But now...

"You will be notified, of course," Majabein cautiously replied. "We realize that you will benefit from taking them. Of course, we would be gravely disappointed if the nature of their mission was exposed, thereby confirming that al Qaeda has roots in Pakistan."

"I surely would not dream of disappointing you," Jadoon replied. And then, "Let's go this way."

They turned onto a narrow street where the babble from the marketplace was muted. Even with the crowd nearby, Jadoon had found a place where they could speak alone and unobserved, for the time being.

"I would like to thank you for your offer," Jadoon said, slipping a hand beneath his jacket, as if scratching at his lower back. "But I'm afraid I must decline."

Decline?

Majabein frowned and said, "I do not—"

"Understand? I thought that you might not."

Jadoon produced a pistol, jammed its muzzle hard against Majabein's ribs and fired. Majabein's body cavity absorbed the shock waves and expanding gases, searing what the bullet did not mangle on its path from lung to lung.

Majabein collapsed to the lumpy pavement. He was already numb below the waist, his chest on fire. He had mere seconds left, but there was time enough for Brigadier Jadoon to whisper in his ear.

"We're finished, you and I," he said. "Sleep well."

THE HIKE FELT more like mountaineering with each forward step. Bolan had done his share of rock climbing and high-altitude training as a member of the Special Forces, and had found some handy applications for it since he'd left the army, but it still drained energy in ways that marching over flat land never could.

It was the simple fact of working against gravity, invisible but inescapable. He'd started with two hundred pounds of bone and muscle, adding another eighty pounds or so of gear and weapons, but two hours into their ascent, it felt like he was carrying a ton.

Still, he kept going, measuring each step to match the one before it, employing his hands when there were outcrops he could use for leverage. In front of him, Gorshani had become a robot, lurching forward as if he were set on automatic pilot.

Bolan kept himself alert in case he had to make a grab for his companion, but so far there had been no need. He thought they had to be drawing near their final destination now, and hoped Gorshani's slowing pace owed more to caution than fatigue.

In confirmation of that thought, Gorshani raised a warning hand, then inched around a shelf of rock and disappeared from view. Bolan crept after him, placing each step with special care, avoiding chips of stone that might go rattling down the mountainside and warn al Qaeda's lookouts of their presence.

Bolan found Gorshani huddled in the shadow of a massive boulder, where the trail broadened, before it narrowed again to something like a scratch mark on the rocky slope. If they moved on from there, they'd definitely have to use the ropes and pitons.

But his guide pointed beyond the boulder now, off to Bolan's right. The Executioner moved closer, craned his neck to peer through a cleft in the stone, and saw a turbaned sentry armed with a Kalashnikov some thirty feet away.

Bolan knew he was looking at al-Bari's first line of defense. There would have been more shooters if the cave was within a pistol shot of where they were sheltered, but the guard meant they were at least closer.

And that guard had to die before they could advance.

Scaling the boulder, even circumnavigating it, would give the sentry time to spot them, turn and fire. A single shot from the Kalashnikov would warn al-Bari's other guards and bring the wrath of God upon them, before they even glimpsed al-Bari's cave.

Bolan set his AKMS rifle on the stony ground and drew his FN Five-seveN pistol. One of his cargo pockets gave up a six-inch suppressor, threaded to fit the weapon's muzzle. Once he had it snug in place, Bolan duck-walked around Gorshani, toward the right side of the boulder that concealed them from the lookout.

It took a minute, but he found the vantage point that he was looking for. Water and wind had worn the boulder smooth, and some calamity in bygone aeons had chiseled a round corner off the stone, tumbling its pieces down to form a series of natural steps. Bolan mounted that rude staircase, testing each step before committing his weight, and soon reached a point where he could observe the guard without being seen.

Thirty feet was close to point-blank range for the Five-seveN's high-powered 5.7 mm cartridge.

All Bolan had to do was aim and fire.

He aimed.

He fired.

12

Lieutenant Colonel Raheem Davi nearly slid out of his jump seat as the M113 APC began to climb the two-lane road ascending Mount Khakwani. He imagined soldiers smirking at him, as he braced himself with one hand on the bulkhead, but his darting glance revealed no secret smiles on any of their faces.

His free hand clutched a submachine gun that he had not fired since he'd completed basic training, though he was confident that he still remembered how to use it. Davi reckoned it would not be necessary, but his memory of the Laghari massacre was clear enough that he would take no chances, where his own survival was concerned.

To that end, Davi had requested backup, but decided not to wait until the extra troops arrived from Peshawar. By that time, Davi's soldiers could secure the cave where al-Bari and his fellow fugitives resided—or, at least, make sure that no intruders could precipitate another bloody slaughter.

Davi stood firm upon one point—if there was any killing to be done that afternoon, his men would do it, on his orders.

As to *who* was killed, well, that remained to be decided by the coming sequence of events.

Davi thanked Allah that the APC had air-conditioning. It was not terribly efficient, granted, but without it he and his assembled troops would all be comatose from heatstroke. As it was, he dreaded stepping out into the broiling sun again, but there was no escaping it.

The higher altitude should help, he thought, although he'd

never fully understood how getting closer to the sun reduced external temperature. There was an issue with endurance, too, in mountain warfare, but he wasn't worried about that.

Once the killing started, Davi knew it would be brisk and brutal, finished within minutes. And the only thing that mattered, in the end, was that Davi be acknowledged as the winner.

He could even bear a minor wound, for the advancement of his reputation and career. It would mean decoration, and a new respect from those who mattered back at headquarters, in Rawalpindi. Davi was not yet sure how to arrange it without mortal danger to himself, but he had always been resourceful. Given half a chance, he'd think of something.

The APC was laboring, but it had been built for heavy work. If old civilian cars could travel over Mount Khakwani, Davi had no doubt that his vehicles could reach their objective. His one drawback, at the moment, was the lack of clear coordinates marking his target.

Never mind.

Al-Bari and the others waited for him, somewhere up ahead, before Khakwani's peak. More to the point, the murderers he sought were headed there, as well, according to the headman of Sanjrani village and the other peasants who had begged Davi to spare the man's life.

This would be his first experience in combat, of a sort, and Davi faced it with a mix of apprehension and excitement. He would not disgrace himself or his command. Above all, he would not permit himself to be surprised.

Weighing the risk of ambush against his desire for warning when they reached al-Bari's lair, Davi turned to the crewman nearest him and said, "Go up and man the turret. Watch for snipers on the mountainside and any sign of habitation."

With a weak "yes, sir," the soldier did as he was told. Davi belatedly discovered that the open hatch nearly negated any benefit from air-conditioning, but he resolved to live with it.

Their target had to be close, now.

He could feel it in his gut, and in his aching rump.

BOLAN'S FIRST SHOT was enough. It put the sentry down without a whimper, though his rifle clattered on the stony mountainside, slipping from lifeless fingers as he fell.

Bolan waited to see if anyone responded to the noise. When no one did, he broke from cover, dragged the lookout's corpse into the shadow of an overhanging ledge, and stripped the magazine from the dead man's Kalashnikov rifle.

One down, and how many left to go?

Gorshani joined him, trailing Bolan now as they advanced along the barest vestige of a trail at a snail's pace. Gorshani's work as Bolan's guide was finished. They had not laid eyes on the al Qaeda sanctuary yet, but posted sentries meant that it was nearby.

From that point on, a soldier led the way.

They met another sentry, sooner than expected. This one was approaching, his movements telegraphed by scraping sounds of boot soles against shale and stone. Perhaps he came to ask the other lookout something or relieve him at his post.

Bolan still held the silenced pistol, with his AKSM slung across his shoulder. He stopped in his tracks and waited for the second target to reveal himself.

Easy. Watch and wait.

A turbaned, bearded figure stepped around the nearest corner of the trail and gaped at Bolan and Gorshani, for perhaps one heartbeat. It was all the time remaining in his life.

Bolan fired one shot, at a range of ten feet. His bullet drilled the stranger's forehead, snapped his head back and sent his turban flapping in the mountain breeze. Bolan removed the magazine from yet another AK, and tucked it inside his web belt as Gorshani dragged the lookout away this time.

Closer, he thought. And after two more minutes on the

narrow track, Bolan heard muffled voices up ahead. Mount Khakwani's acoustics played tricks with his ears, but he guessed that the speakers were no more than fifty feet distant.

Gorshani heard them, too, and nodded in response to Bolan's arched eyebrow. The Pakistani edged closer, cocking his head to pick out words and phrases, listened for a full minute or more, before he whispered a response to Bolan.

"They are talking about women. Sharing prostitutes to save their money. Nothing serious."

"How many?" Bolan asked.

"I only hear two voices, but if more are listening…" Gorshani left it hanging, finished with a helpless shrug.

And he was right, of course. It was the same with soldiers—hell, with men—whenever they had time to kill. Some guys were talkers, while others stood around and soaked it up, grinning. It didn't matter if they thought the ones doing the talking were outrageous liars. Tuning in was almost mandatory.

"We have to take them," Bolan said.

Gorshani nodded grim acceptance of the obvious.

Raising his pistol, Bolan said, "I've still got eighteen rounds left. I'll go first. Fire only as a last resort."

Another nod.

Bracing his FN Five-seveN in a two-handed grip, Bolan stepped out to meet his enemies.

AKRAM BEN ABD al-Bari felt a headache starting at his left temple. Restraining an impulse to grimace, he laid down the sheaf of photographs that he had been examining—a military base filled with Crusaders, outside Kandahar, Afghanistan—and told Ra'id Ibn Rashad, "I need to step outside."

Frowning at the expression on al-Bari's face, Rashad inquired, "Are you not well?"

"Fresh air, a little sun, I'll be all right," al-Bari said.

Each time he rose from sitting on the stony floor, it seemed to take more time and effort than it had before. Further proof that he was aging, and al-Bari realized that living in a cave was not a recipe for aging gracefully.

He had resigned himself to spending his last days on this mountain, thinking of it as a sacrifice to Allah and jihad. The idea did not please al-Bari, but he knew discomfort was the very least one should expect from martyrdom.

Sometimes, when weariness oppressed al-Bari, he imagined strapping on a Semtex vest and driving down the mountain, seeking out a target of his own, and wafting off to Paradise on roiling clouds of fire. It seemed more fitting, somehow, for a lifelong warrior to obliterate himself in battle, rather than wasting away in a hole in a mountain.

But he was needed. The top man himself decreed it.

Still, perhaps one day...

Al-Bari was twenty feet from the cave's entrance, passing a cluster of guards who'd averted their eyes as a sign of respect, when he heard the first gunshot. It sent a jolt of pure adrenaline through his veins, awakening the ancient fight-or-flight instinct, but al-Bari had time to do neither.

Hard on the heels of the first shot, several automatic weapons opened fire outside the cave, followed an instant later by the crash of an explosion. Its shock wave staggered al-Bari, while dust from the rocky ceiling above him speckled his turban, shoulders and beard.

One of his guards grabbed al-Bari's arm and pulled him back, deeper into the cavern, while most of the others ran to join the fight outside the entrance. As al-Bari let himself be led away, he wondered who had come to kill him, whether they were skilled and numerous enough to do the job.

A sudden image of the cave collapsing, trapping him forever underground, froze the man in his tracks. He tugged against the bodyguard's restraining grip and almost bolted toward the sunlight he could just barely see, through a swirl of dust and smoke.

"Master," the guard said, "you must seek shelter!"

"Yes," he said, then grabbed the man's rifle, pivoted while twisting sharply, and disarmed him with an ease that left al-Bari wondering how the young man had survived this long.

"*You* go, seek shelter if you must," al-Bari told his startled soldier. "I will face my enemies."

THE FIRST SOUNDS of gunfire were distant, barely echoes in the confines of the APC, but Raheem Davi still heard them over the sound of the vehicle's engine. He bolted upright from his seat, groping for balance with his free hand on the bulkhead, as he shouted orders at the APC's driver.

"Faster! It's started! Get me there right now!"

Davi turned toward the turret gunner, only visible from the waist down, and gave a sharp yank on his trouser leg. The gunner ducked to face him.

"Yes, sir?"

"What do you see?"

"Nothing yet, sir. I—"

"Keep watch, then!" Davi raged, feeling the other soldiers' eyes upon him as he lurched and staggered in the narrow aisle between their seats.

The crack of an explosion slapped his eardrums, and the sounds of automatic fire redoubled. Davi knew they had to be close, now, and it suddenly occurred to him that they should not approach the battleground blindly.

Before he had a chance to speak, the turret gunner called down to him, "Sir! I see them!"

"Who?" Davi demanded, calling from below.

"Guerrillas!"

Davi rounded on the driver, shouting, "Stop! Open the cargo hatch!"

The APC shuddered to a halt, brakes groaning with the effort, and the driver flipped a dashboard switch that instantly produced a whining sound from the rear of the vehicle. The broad cargo gate lowered smoothly, rather than dropping to slam on the ground, leaving Davi to mutter and curse while he waited.

At last, it was open, and Davi bawled orders to his men, herding them before him out the vehicle's armored womb. Behind them, the second APC had also stopped, and in another moment it was also spilling troops onto the narrow roadway.

Bringing up the rear, Davi risked a look around the APC's left flank and saw two riflemen in robes and turbans, retreating as fast as they could over boulders and crags. The sounds of battle came from farther up the mountain, but not much farther. Say, another fifty yards or so.

"Get after those two!" Davi ordered. "Find out who's shooting and put a stop to it! Go, now!"

His soldiers moved out, cautiously, while Davi leaned back inside the APC's open maw and issued further orders. "Close this up and follow them," he told the driver. Then, he gave a last shout to the turret gunner, "Cover them. I want supporting fire on any hostile targets!"

Having done the best he could, Lieutenant Colonel Davi ran to catch up with his troops. They had a lead on him by now, as he'd foreseen, which meant that they would be the first to meet with any risk, while he brought up the rear.

Davi was new to combat, but he was not stupid. He intended to come out of this alive, victorious, and with enough prestige to carry him through to a promotion.

Flicking off his rifle's safety, he made sure the weapon had a live round in its chamber and its magazine was firmly seated. Sweating from the brutal heat already, and perhaps from his anxiety, Davi ran toward the din of combat just ahead.

GORSHANI HAD begun to think Matt Cooper was invincible. When Cooper stepped around the outcropping, Gorshani on his heels, there had been three sentries instead of two, but it appeared to make no difference.

Rapid-firing with his pistol, the big American had dropped all three of them before they could react. He swept from right to left, pop-pop-pop, and the turbaned strangers had died with dazed expressions on their faces.

One had gotten a slug through his left cheek, the next above an eyebrow, and the third below his bearded jawline, spouting crimson from a severed artery. They fell almost together, not quite touching, sprawled in boneless postures of death. Gorshani had relaxed his index finger on the trigger of his rifle, realizing that his help was not required.

"This way," Bolan instructed him, and set off without waiting to see if Gorshani would obey.

Of course, he followed the soldier from sudden death to ever greater danger, and what other choice was there? He could not descend the mountain now and leave him to fight alone, although it seemed to be the tall man's preference.

Gorshani knew they had to be near the cave, and so was not surprised when Cooper flagged him to a halt, peering around one final outcropping. Below them, at some distance, lay the only road traversing Mount Khakwani, and Gorshani half imagined he could hear vehicles climbing it, right now.

Another moment, inching forward in response to Cooper's silent gesture, and before he even saw the cave, Gorshani definitely heard vehicles, large ones, two of them at least. He guessed that lorries would not come this way, preferring lower passes, and that made him worry all the more.

The cave's mouth was approximately seven feet in height, and twice that in width. It was disguised, after a fashion, by a hanging tarp painted to match the mountain's dark-gray stone. The tarp was pulled aside, permitting riflemen to traipse in and out of the cave, unimpeded.

"This is it," Bolan advised. "We won't get in without a fight, and it sounds like company's coming."

His nod toward the road confirmed Gorshani's assessment, and he gave a curt nod in return.

"I am ready," Gorshani said.

"Short bursts," Bolan told him. "Make them count."

And in a sudden rush of movement, he was gone, charging the cave's mouth and its complement of guards. His AKMS had no silencer, and they were done with anything resembling stealth.

Gorshani saw the first guard fall, his arms outflung, rifle cartwheeling through the air, and then he was rushing after Cooper, picking out a target of his own.

Far to the right he spotted a gunner with a long face, gray streaks in his beard, although he did not seem that old. The man was raising his Kalashnikov, swinging around toward Cooper, when Gorshani hit him with a 3-round burst and dropped him where he stood.

There had been eight or nine guards visible when Cooper had broken from cover. Half of them were down now, and the rest were dodging back into the cave behind them, firing as they went. Gorshani hunched his shoulders, heard their bullets slicing through the mountain air around him, but there was no time for him to be afraid.

He caught one of the sentries running, stitched him from his hip to his armpit and sent him tumbling through a kind of clumsy shoulder roll that ended with the runner stretched out on his back, still.

To his left, Gorshani was aware of Cooper ducking, dodging, moving ever forward, firing short bursts all the while. His rifle had a larger magazine, requiring fewer reloadings, but Gorshani guessed that his own clip still held ten or twelve cartridges.

And he would make the most of them.

Gorshani fired into the shadows of the cave's entrance, thought he saw a human figure lurch and stagger, but he wasn't positive. More fire was coming from the cave now, forcing him off to his right, where tumbled boulders offered an uncertain sanctuary.

From behind him, he heard Cooper shout, "Fire in the hole!" Immediately afterward, Gorshani recognized the cough of the GP-25 grenade launcher, followed almost instantly by an explosion from the cave. A cloud of mingled dust and smoke spewed from the entrance, while within, the cries of wounded men echoed from the rugged walls of stone.

Gorshani found a boulder large enough to shelter him and dropped behind it, flicking nervous glances back and forth between Cooper and the smoky entrance to the cave. Somehow, he knew that they had to get inside to find al-Bari and the others, but he did not see how it would be possible.

And then he heard the sound of heavy vehicles approaching on the narrow road. Gorshani peered in that direction, could not see them yet, but knew that he would be exposed to anyone approaching from his flank.

No time to move, he thought. No time for anything.

Except, perhaps, to die.

AKRAM AL-BARI had considered plunging headlong into battle with the unknown enemy, but the explosion at the cave's mouth had suggested a more useful and fulfilling course of action. Thus, he had retreated, carrying his captured rifle, to the chamber where munitions were stockpiled.

The squarish room held crates of ammunition and explosives. There was enough, he supposed, to hold a small army at bay for several weeks, but siege warfare had long ago gone out of style. A modern enemy could burn or gas his soldiers in their lair, or simply seal off the entrance and go away, leaving al-Bari and his men to starve and waste away in darkness without end.

Al-Bari had a different plan.

He found a pile of cheap load-bearing vests, with all-over pockets, and selected one that seemed to be about his size. Next, he began to stuff its pouch pockets with oblong bricks of Semtex, relishing the scent of marzipan that had been added by the manufacturer, specifically to aid against detection of the odorless plastique.

When he had filled all but one of the pockets with Semtex, al-Bari placed a dry-cell battery in the final pouch and fastened slim wires to its terminals. He left those dangling as he slipped into the vest and buttoned it, testing its weight.

The ten Semtex blocks, weighing about twenty-two pounds, plus the fat battery, pulled al-Bari's shoulders down a little, but he didn't mind. After all, he would only have to bear the load for a few more minutes.

Blasting caps were kept well away from the Semtex, in small plastic boxes. Al-Bari knew where they were, and he took his time pressing one into each cake of explosives, setting them deeply for maximum ignition. The final wiring was the tricky part, connecting the various caps with peripheral wires, bringing them all together with the handheld detonator, and finally attaching the battery's leads once he had everything else arranged to his liking.

The al Qaeda honcho held the detonator in his left hand, lifting the liberated Kalashnikov with his right, but then decided the gun was too heavy and left it behind.

He wondered where Ra'id Ibn Rashad had gone, then put it out of mind. There was no secondary exit from the cave, although construction had been underway on two escape tunnels, almost from the moment al-Bari had moved in. But it had proved tough going, and now they would never be finished.

Goodbye, old friend, wherever you are, he thought.

The top man might be angry, but in time he would agree with al-Bari's decision. Capture meant shame, perhaps torture—and even disgrace, if he broke from the pain.

But sacrifice was beautiful.

Wearing a rare expression of contentment on his face, al-Bari turned back toward the cave's mouth, where the battle raged. With each step, he felt more content.

Each step brought him another pace closer to Paradise.

BOLAN HEARD THE DRONE of an advancing heavy vehicle behind him, creeping up the narrow mountain road below al-Bari's cave. Those wouldn't be al Qaeda reinforcements coming to the rescue in an APC, which meant that Pakistani soldiers were about to join the party.

The Executioner was swiftly running out of time, and he hadn't even glimpsed al-Bari yet.

Bolan had known there was no realistic hope of finding his primary targets on the mountain slope. The odds against it had been astronomical, and he'd already primed himself to seek al-Bari and Rashad belowground in the murky labyrinth of caverns, but the military presence closing in behind him threatened even that approach.

He had enough time to unload a few more 40 mm rounds before the troops arrived, but Bolan knew those charges wouldn't be enough to seal the entrance and entomb his enemies.

It came down to the soldiers now, and to the fact that Bolan couldn't know if they were here simply to kill him, or to save al-Bari and his minions in the bargain. If they weren't committed to protecting the al Qaeda base of operations, then—

He got his answer when a couple of al-Bari's riflemen, apparently bypassed when Bolan and Gorshani had made their move against the cave, fired on the troops advancing from below. A heartbeat later, Bolan heard the unmistakable reply of .50-caliber machine guns hammering the mountainside, joined instantly by what seemed to be dozens of Kalashnikovs.

Whatever their commander's motive when he brought them up the mountain, hostile fire had moved the soldiers to respond in kind, and there could be no turning back. Al-Bari's men had set the tone for what had to follow, turned the troops against them in an eye blink—and perhaps, just maybe, aided Bolan in the process.

Would al-Bari and Rashad surrender, when they found themselves outgunned and trapped inside their cave? Could

Bolan and Gorshani now withdraw, while there was time, and leave the mopping up to other hands?

Bolan was undecided, when he saw a white-garbed figure shuffle to the entrance of the cave, upright and seemingly oblivious to bullets rattling all around him. Even through the swirl of dust and smoke, he recognized al-Bari and was sighting down the barrel of his AKSM when the man raised one hand overhead, wires trailing from his fist down to a bulky vest.

Al-Bari shouted something Bolan didn't understand. But Bolan knew what was coming, as he called a warning to Gorshani—likely wasted, drowned in the racket of gunfire—and lurched back under cover of the boulders close by.

The blast verged on apocalyptic, shattering the arch of stone above al-Bari's head and upraised arm. The mountainside buckled, then thundered down to bury him and his assembled guards, spewing a massive cloud of dust and shattered stone that rolled downhill to blind the cautiously advancing Pakistani troops.

Somehow, Gorshani came to Bolan through the smoke and thunder, limping, barely clinging to his rifle, gagging on the dust. Their downhill track was painfully obscured, forcing the two of them to grope their way along, slipping and scrabbling in their haste, while echoes of the numbing blast merged with the crackle of ongoing gunfire, soldiers and the few surviving sentries killing one another in a last spasm of violence.

Bolan and his guide were far from safe, but it was downhill all the way.

Just like the road to hell.

13

Army Headquarters, Rawalpindi

Lieutenant Colonel Raheem Davi willed himself to sit still in the small waiting room. A low table spread with magazines of military interest stood before him, but he could not focus on their titles, much less sit there and pretend to read the articles.

Behind his practiced poker face, a storm of contradictory emotions raged. Davi was proud, of course, for having won a victory with only two men lost. But there was also apprehension, edging closer to outright fear with each tick of the wall clock.

Would he be punished, after all, for what the terrorists had done to themselves? Would someone higher up the chain of rank, or in the halls of government, resent the bloody dissolution of al Qaeda headquarters in Pakistan?

It was a possibility.

Worse yet, Davi had no proof that any of the dead on Mount Khakwani were the men he had set out to kill or capture in the first place. They might never find Hussein Gorshani's body, even if it was among the others. As for the foreign soldier, Davi hadn't seen anyone who looked British or American, but he'd been late arriving on the scene. In fact, he had missed the final blast, only feeling its shock waves and viewing its aftermath.

The cleaning up, as far as he could tell without experience, had been routine. A few guerrillas had been spared by the explosion, trapped outside the cave that had become their master's tomb. They had fought to the death, killing two of his men, but the outcome was never in doubt.

A quick search of the mountainside revealed no living stragglers, and Davi had contacted Brigadier Jadoon by satellite phone, before he radioed the news to Peshawar. Despite the bloodshed and excitement, he had kept his personal priorities in line.

The rest of it had been like riding on a whirlwind. First, a statement to the officer in charge at Peshawar, and then a flight back to the Rawalpindi airfield. There was time to don his new dress uniform, before his audience with Brigadier Jadoon, but even that was rushed.

Such trouble just to sit and wait like some lowly job applicant, while Jadoon dawdled and delayed.

At last, the *havildar* in charge of Jadoon's office summoned Davi, leading him along the short hallway to Jadoon's private sanctum. Davi noted that the *havildar* did not salute him, wondering if he should draw some inference from that. Perhaps he should make an excuse—the men's room, anything—and flee the building, find a vehicle outside, run for his life.

But Brigadier Jadoon was smiling as he greeted Davi, offering his right hand in a rare gesture of greeting. Davi shook it gratefully, but remained on edge as Jadoon steered him to a chair facing the brigadier's large desk.

Jadoon sat down behind the desk, leaned forward on his elbows and said, "So, you come home a hero from the wars."

It was a time for cautious modesty, even if feigned. "Hardly a hero, sir," Davi replied.

"You were successful, were you not?"

"Yes, sir. I was."

"In all respects?" Jadoon inquired.

There was the trap, yawning before him. Was it already too late to sidestep, or should Davi plunge headlong into its maw?

"Sir," he replied, "as you're aware, a great explosion sealed the cave. It will require a team of army engineers to open it, and even they may fail. Under those circumstances, and considering your urgent summons, I did not complete a full inspection of the site."

"Meaning?"

"Simply, that we have not identified Hussein Gorshani's body, sir. Or that of his anonymous companion."

Jadoon leaned back in his chair, not quite relaxing, as he asked, "How confident are you, Raheem, that you have solved our problem?"

Now came the backroom diplomacy, like walking barefoot on a razor's edge.

"Sir, I believe Hussein Gorshani and the foreigner are dead," Davi replied. "But even if I am mistaken, they have nothing more to do in Pakistan. Their mission, as we have determined, was to kill Akram Ben Abd al-Bari and his aides. That task has been completed."

"So?"

"Sir, even if the subjects are alive, the foreigner can only seek to flee the country. I submit that he had to take Gorshani with him, since the traitor's name and face are known to us. He can no longer safely live in Pakistan. We do, however, have another chance to catch them at the border, *if* they live."

"And if we miss them, somehow?" Jadoon asked.

"Sir, who will ever know it? If the Brits or the Americans were certain of al-Bari's whereabouts, they would have sent cruise missiles, blown the mountain down around him and announced their triumph to the world on CNN. Sending a single man tells us they were uncertain."

Once again, the brigadier said, "So?"

"Remember Libya? Baghdad? Afghanistan? These Westerners love toys. Their bombs and missiles all have cameras mounted on them, to broadcast their final moments and proclaim their accuracy as a gloating show of force. With one man on the ground, hunted, perhaps already slain, what do they have to show? Where is their proof?"

Jadoon considered that, his lips forming the bare suggestion of a smile.

"You may be right, Raheem. I hope so, for your sake... and mine."

"Sir?"

"I am recommending your promotion to full colonel. I am also recommending the Sitara-e-Jurat."

Davi blinked twice at that. The Sitara-e-Jurat was Pakistan's third-highest military decoration for gallant and distinguished combat service.

Davi found his voice at last. "Sir, thank you! I can only say—"

"Say nothing, for the moment," Jadoon cautioned. "There are some—perhaps you even know them—who are not exactly overjoyed by the results of your excursion. I suspect they will be bashful about openly attacking you, but they have sharp knives and long memories."

"I understand, sir."

"Do you? Well, perhaps. I'm turning in the paperwork for your promotion and the rest tomorrow, but you know that these things can't be rushed."

"Yes, sir."

"Meanwhile, complete your field report and have it on my desk by noon."

"Yes, sir!"

"You've done good work, Davi. But be on guard against those who may disagree."

THE DRIVE to Rawalpindi had been nerve-racking, but Bolan and Gorshani had pulled it off without a hitch. They took turns driving, but Gorshani did the shopping, bought the gasoline, and handled any situations that required a dialog in Urdu or Pashto.

The easy part was getting lost among the city's three million inhabitants. Bolan stayed close to Gorshani, slouching in his peasant garb and headgear to reduce his height, and spent as much time as he could inside their stolen car. Aided by the days of stubble on his cheeks and jaw, the sun on Bolan's olive skin had made him dark enough to pass a cursory inspection.

Gorshani found it hard to settle down, after their battle on the mountain, but he listened well enough when Bolan told him that nervous attitude could get both of them killed. He proved to be a decent actor, overall.

But he was adamant about remaining in his homeland after Bolan finished his one last job and left.

"I'll find some way to manage it," he said, when Bolan told him for the third time that it was a reckless, suicidal plan.

"They have your name, now," Bolan had reminded him. "Somebody in Sanjrani gave you up. That means the state police and military have your house, whatever was inside it—everything. It's why we had to ditch the SUV."

"I can't blame anyone for that," Gorshani said.

"That's not my point. Forgive them if you want to, but you can't forget. You can't pretend that everything's gone back to how it was two days ago."

"Before you came," Gorshani said.

"Don't even *try* guilt-tripping me," Bolan replied. "You volunteered. Al-Bari and the rest were sitting on their mountaintop for years."

"Of course. And now they're gone. I think my country's leaders will decide it is a good thing."

"Good or bad," Bolan said, "they'll still want someone to answer for the soldiers."

"But, when your work is completed—"

"Nothing will have changed," Bolan said, cutting through the wishful thinking. "You'll have the same rulers in place who let al-Bari come here in the first place. And your name will still be on Islamabad's most-wanted list."

"You ask me to abandon everything."

"You *have* abandoned everything. It's gone. Who do you think answered the phone at your apartment when you called last night? A burglar? Someone from the community welcome committee?"

"They will change their minds," Gorshani answered stubbornly. "I will allow the dust to settle, as you say, and—"

"The dust will settle on your grave if they get hold of you. You're living in a fantasy if you think otherwise."

"You do not know my people, Matt."

"I know they've spent two days working overtime to kill us. Now, you're saying all will be forgiven if you wait a little while. It doesn't track."

Gorshani remained silent.

"Look, I'm not saying that you have to settle in the States. Maybe the Agency can set you up some kind of deal in India or Afghanistan. It won't be home, but you've worn out your welcome here."

"Again, I have to disagree."

Bolan was tired of arguing the point. "It's your call," he agreed reluctantly. "But help me find our man before you stick your head inside the noose, all right?"

"With pleasure."

"Are you sure about the home address?"

"It's classified, of course. But, yes, I trust my source."

"You said it's near a school?"

"Correct. The Gordon College, off Liaquat Road."

"Not a restricted neighborhood?" Bolan inquired.

"Our car should not be stopped," Gorshani said. "Though if we were walking on the street, perhaps we would be questioned."

"We should look for guards, though."

"Under the present circumstances, certainly."

It was nearing dusk, but they had some time to spare.

"Let's make a pass," Bolan said, "then hang back and give him time to come home from the office."

"If I'm wrong, and we are stopped…"

"I'll handle it," Bolan said.

Hoping that, if they were intercepted, it would by a military operation, not police.

Some rules he wouldn't break at any price, including his life, or his driver's.

"I suppose," Gorshani said, "the good news is that they will not expect us here."

"Let's hope not," Bolan said.

But he was always ready for the absolute worst-case scenario.

It was the only way he'd stayed alive this long.

ARMY HEADQUARTERS in Rawalpindi was located south of the Lei Nala River, sprawling over several square miles bounded by Taimur Road on the north and Sarwar Road on the south. Landmarks on the outskirts of the complex included a medical college and a slaughterhouse, a Christian clubhouse and a squalid shantytown, plus the gleaming offices of Citibank and American Express.

Rawalpindi was all things to all men.

Brigadier Bahaar Jadoon left his office at half-past seven o'clock on a wearying day, exhausted from jumping through hoops to please his superiors. Jadoon believed that he had finally put their worst fears to rest, but it was possible that some of them would call throughout the night with fresh concerns.

Mostly about themselves.

As Jadoon had expected, no voices had been raised in anguish at the violent passing of Akram Ben Abd al-Bari or his aides. His superiors' chief concern was that al-Bari and his men had died in Pakistan, after so many years of stern denials that al Qaeda had any foothold there.

Offsetting that concern, as he had told Raheem Davi, had been the way they had died. It provided America with no concrete proof of the event. And furthermore, if evidence *did* surface, politicians in Islamabad could claim al-Bari and his men had been killed by Pakistani troops.

For half a dozen of them, it would even be the truth.

As for Hussein Gorshani and the missing foreigner, he was content to let them *stay* missing, if they had common sense enough to disappear.

Jadoon's rank qualified him for a driver. His chauffeur was a fresh-faced *havildar* newly promoted, the chevrons still bright and stiff on his sleeves. The young man snapped to attention as Jadoon approached his staff car, executing a crisp salute before he opened the brigadier's door.

Dusk was still a half hour away as they drove north along Murree Road, then west on Taimur Road to reach the north-south artery of Gawal Mandi Road. From there, it was a crawl through Gawal Mandi to a bridge spanning the Lei Nala, and across Liaquat Road to the Naya Mohalla district where Jadoon resided.

His home was on the small side, but the neighborhood was quiet, peaceful and well patrolled. Most days, there were no beggars on the streets, and Jadoon normally had few concerns about security.

This day, of course, was different.

It would have seemed peculiar for an officer of Jadoon's rank if he had not assigned soldiers to guard his home during such troubled times. Accordingly, he had selected four men— the bare minimum, for such a detail—to stake out his house and watch it through the night, and perhaps into tomorrow.

After that, Jadoon reasoned, it would be safe to drop the pose and go back to business as usual.

He had expected some sense of relief over al-Bari's death, but now that it had actually happened he felt an urge to shout and dance with joy. Jadoon had lived under al-Bari's thumb so long, he had become accustomed to the numbing border-line depression that accompanied incessant fear of ridicule, disgrace, arrest and prison.

All that had been obliterated within a few brief, violent moments. And the most delicious irony of all was that it appeared al-Bari had done it to himself.

A true fanatic to the end, Jadoon thought. Perhaps afraid that if he had been arrested, he would have been coerced into exposing crucial secrets of al Qaeda.

And quite right, too.

Al-Bari, in a cage, would ultimately have to have been released or placed on trial. In either case, the CIA, Mossad and Britain's MI-6 would have all been clamoring for custody, prepared to use whatever means necessary to unlock the secrets in al-Bari's head. Nothing but the Apocalypse would have ever set him free, once he was locked away. What better way to die, from a zealot's viewpoint, than to kill himself and take some of his enemies along with him?

Praise Allah for small favors, Jadoon thought.

One of Jadoon's guards waited at the curb outside his home. The driver would have called ahead to warn the soldiers he was coming, have them on alert and looking sharp when Jadoon stepped out of his car. What would his neighbors think, seeing soldiers and guns around his house for the first time?

Jadoon dismissed the question as irrelevant.

It made no difference what they thought.

Jadoon thanked his driver, returned the *havildar's* salute without enthusiasm and brushed past the guard on the sidewalk. The guard saluted him, as well, then turned his scrutiny back toward the quiet residential street.

There would be two more soldiers in the backyard, which overlooked a semiwild ravine, and one—perhaps another *havildar*—on roving duty to make sure the others did not fall asleep through the long night ahead.

Jadoon would leave the back door open for them, granting access to the kitchen and the lavatory. Coffee and a toilet were the basics, and would be considered luxuries in portions of the North-West Frontier Province where so many other soldiers had been killed over the past two days.

All finished now, Jadoon thought, as he let himself into his house.

He could forget about the past—or the worst parts of it, anyway. He could erase the memory of one grim indiscretion that had bound him to al-Bari and the other bastards, as a kind of slave to their demands. That was behind him now.

It had occurred to Brigadier Jadoon that in the weeks and months ahead, other spokesmen for al Qaeda might surface to whisper a reminder of his crimes—jerk on the leash and bring him back to heel. It was a possibility, of course, but having finally tasted freedom, Jadoon was not inclined to give it up without a fight.

He would demand to see the evidence, brook no refusal. He might surprise the blackmailers next time.

Assuming that there was a next time.

On the brighter side, perhaps the proof of Jadoon's debt had lived only within al-Bari's mind—or buried in the cavern where he'd died.

Jadoon was determined to be kept well-informed, if excavation at the site resumed. Until then, he was free.

A cause to celebrate.

Jadoon moved toward his study, where he kept a few wine bottles locked away from prying eyes. Allah would certainly forgive him in this instance, he believed, for having just a sip of alcohol.

Or maybe two.

He had not felt so free in ages, and was not about to let the feeling slip away just yet.

HUSSEIN GORSHANI parked his stolen car on the campus of Gordon College, where he was fairly sure it would be overlooked for the night. And though he did not have the proper parking decals, Gorshani deemed a citation more likely than a tow-away.

In any case, if they returned and found the car missing, they could acquire another one without great difficulty.

If they were alive.

Matt Cooper's work in Rawalpindi struck Gorshani as an afterthought, perhaps something conceived in haste, but he could see the logic to it, if he tried to think like an American. Bahaar Jadoon had certainly worked on al Qaeda's behalf. What was the point of killing off Akram Ben Abd al-Bari and the rest if Cooper left their greatest ally in the army standing by to serve another group of terrorists?

They had established that Jadoon was under guard. A quick drive past his home had settled that. One soldier on the street, for show, and Cooper reckoned that there had to be several more stationed around the property to cover all approaches.

At the rear, they found that Jadoon's small lot overlooked a rugged gully overgrown with weeds, saplings and wild-flowers. A fence guarded the brigadier's backyard against invasion by wild animals or tramps, but it would not keep out determined prowlers.

Cooper carried most of their weapons in a duffel bag, leaving Gorshani with only his pistol tucked under his belt, in the small of his back. Gorshani wished he had a silencer to fit it, but he compensated by repeating Cooper's orders in his head: you're backup, this time. Stay clear, if you can.

It seemed absurd, after all that they'd been through together since Cooper dropped out of the sky, but Gorshani meant to follow those instructions.

If he could.

So far, nothing about his mission with the tall American had gone according to plan. Instead of simply guiding Cooper and translating local dialects, Gorshani had been sucked into the midst of bloody action against soldiers and terrorists alike.

And, based on their behavior toward the common people of his homeland, was there really any difference between the two? He had to wonder.

They found the weed-choked gully just as dusk descended upon the city. Pausing while light traffic passed, they left the pavement and scrambled down a slope that crumbled underfoot, until tall grass and tumbleweeds surrounded them, scraping against their trousers, tangling around their boots.

"Watch out for snakes," he warned Cooper.

"Will do."

Despite Rawalpindi's teeming population, wildlife still inhabited some portions of the city, and this gully seemed ideal for kraits, cobras, even the dreaded Russell's viper.

It would be the crowning irony, Gorshani thought, to have a lowly reptile kill him after all he had survived of late, dealing with lethal human beings.

But they met no snakes along the way. Cooper found his mark and cautiously began to climb another dirt embankment, some three hundred yards from where they'd entered the ravine. Standing below and watching him, Gorshani recognized the fence that ringed Bahaar Jadoon's backyard.

So, here we are, he thought.

And doggedly began to climb.

THE BACKYARD GUARDS were easy. Bolan found them smoking on a patio behind Bahaar Jadoon's house, underneath a yellow light designed to ward off flying insects. Trusting in the light to spoil their night vision, he cut the chain-link fence instead of scaling it—less noise—and tied the flap open with twists of wire to make it simpler for Gorshani, bringing up the rear.

When he was thirty feet from contact, still outside the pool of yellow light that bathed the patio, he drew the black Five-seveN pistol. Even with its fully loaded magazine, the gun weighed barely a pound and a half, thanks in equal part to its plastic grip and the fact that its twenty 5.7 mm rounds weighed only half as much as standard 9 mm Parabellum cartridges.

Recoil was likewise reduced from the typical niner, despite

the 5.7 mm's powder load, which enabled the bullets to penetrate Kevlar. Also, like the military M-16 projectiles, they were designed for maximum internal damage without a hollow point round's expansion or the explosive fragmentation of a frangible bullet.

Bolan thought he heard Gorshani entering the yard behind him, but the lookouts didn't seem to notice. They were busy whispering about something apparently very enthralling, distracted from the last assignment they would ever have.

The soldier on the Executioner's right posed the greater danger, with an AK tucked under his arm, while his companion wore his rifle slung, its muzzle pointed toward the ground. It was a sloppy attitude, and this time fatal.

Bolan squeezed the pistol's trigger twice, producing two muffled coughing sounds, and watched the sentries crumple to the ground where they stood. The takedown had made some noise, particularly the weapons rattling on the patio, so Bolan waited, frozen, to confront any response.

It took a moment, but he soon heard another soldier coming from the south side of the house, pushing through shrubbery and calling out what sounded like a question. The new arrival didn't shout, taking care not to disturb his boss inside unnecessarily, but the tone was unmistakably urgent.

No response came from the dead men.

A noncom wearing chevrons on his sleeve burst into view on Bolan's right and skidded to a halt on the grass. He saw the bodies first, then swung around toward Bolan's shadow-shape beyond the light, but never had a chance to focus on his killer.

Bolan fired another nearly silent round and dropped the sergeant of the guard before he had a chance to reach for his holstered sidearm. By the time the Executioner's third spent cartridge hit the ground, Gorshani stood beside him, scanning the three corpses for a latent sign of life.

One sentry left, but Bolan guessed that he was stuck out front until someone relieved him. Nothing that had happened in the backyard would have reached his ears, or else the fourth man would be lying with his comrades, leaking blood and brains.

The house was Bolan's next challenge.

With military guards in place, would there be an alarm? He checked the sliding glass door that gave access to the patio and saw no evidence that it was wired. That didn't prove it wasn't, but he would have to take a chance.

He gambled that the sentries on the patio would not have been encouraged to relieve themselves in the brigadier's yard. With that reasoning, Bolan tested the sliding door with his free hand and felt it move along its runners.

Seconds later, he was standing in the air-conditioned house, feeling the sweat chill on his skin. Gorshani entered behind him and stepped to his left. They kept a wall at their backs while they studied the room.

It was some kind of parlor, with chairs and a sofa arranged for a simultaneous view of the yard and the king-size TV set. Bolan didn't know what kind of programs an Islamic brigadier enjoyed, but whatever his viewing pleasure, Jadoon had seen his last broadcast.

Bolan followed a dim light, entering the parlor, then proceeded into a kitchen, where a stocky man wearing a T-shirt and boxers sat at a smallish round table, spooning ice cream from a carton. His back was turned to Bolan, but it hardly mattered. Bolan didn't know Jadoon's face, hadn't seen his photograph or read his file.

He simply knew that Jadoon and al-Bari had collaborated to perpetuate a reign of terror, orchestrated from al Qaeda's sanctuary here, in Pakistan. It was enough, but Bolan had to know that this was his intended target, not some hired hand chowing down while Jadoon snoozed in his bedroom.

"Bahaar Jadoon?" he asked.

The man's head whipped around, smearing a streak of chocolate across his right cheek from his upraised spoon. He looked at the gun in Bolan's hand and froze, but responded with a question of his own that was gibberish to Bolan's ears.

"You speak English?"

"Of course," the seated man replied.

"You *are* Bahaar Jadoon?"

"I'm *Brigadier* Jadoon," the officer replied, as if his rank would save him, sitting in his skivvies with a spoonful of melting ice cream in hand.

"Just so there's no mistake," Bolan said.

"I know you," Jadoon said. "You are the foreigner. Is the traitor here, as well?"

"I'm here," Gorshani said from somewhere behind Bolan. "And I say *you* are the traitor, joining with al Qaeda to betray our homeland."

"This won't help you," Jadoon said, addressing both of them. "Kill me, and you'll still be trapped in Pakistan. Where will you hide? For how long?"

"That's my concern, not yours," Bolan said, already tiring of the dialogue.

"You should be concerned," Jadoon said. "Spare me, and I can help you—"

Then Jadoon made a fatal mistake—he reached for the gun in the waistband of his boxers. Bolan's bullet drilled through the brigadier's forehead and churned its vicious way through gray matter, coming to rest against his occipital bone. Jadoon managed a final blink in parting, then slumped over with his right cheek resting on the open ice cream carton.

"We're out of here," he told Gorshani. "Same way we came in, but twice as quiet."

Despite Bolan preparing him for this moment, explaining why they'd come, Gorshani still looked slightly dazed. Or was that anger, frustrated by removal of its target?

"Leaving now," Bolan informed him, brushing past Gorshani toward the parlor and their exit on the right. Before he reached the sliding door, he heard the Pakistani following.

"I would have done it," Gorshani said, once they'd cleared the fence and scrambled down into the weeds.

"I had the silencer," Bolan reminded him.

"Of course."

When they were halfway down the length of the ravine, Gorshani stopped and said, "He's right, you know. You're both right. I have no home, now. There's nowhere I can hide."

"Not here," Bolan replied. "At least, not now." Lifting the sat phone from his belt, he said, "I'll book a second ticket on the next flight out."

"They will be watching all the airlines," Gorshani said.

"Not the one I have in mind," Bolan replied.

Epilogue

The hardest part of Jack Grimaldi's job, once he'd received the sat-phone call, was staying grounded in Afghanistan while Bolan drove from Rawalpindi to their designated pickup point.

It was about 180 miles—three hours over decent highways, driving at a normal sixty miles per hour, but Grimaldi guessed the roads Bolan would travel weren't on par with any U.S. freeway. Another drawback was the need to keep a low profile, and not attract the soldiers and police who had to be swarming everywhere, like driver ants, throughout the North-West Frontier Province.

Anyway, the waiting was a bitch.

Grimaldi's second-hardest job would be extracting Bolan and his unexpected ride-along if they were spotted, either on radar or by the troops who had to be hunting Bolan, even now.

Pickups were always harder than deliveries.

At the start of his mission, Bolan had jumped from a high-flying fixed-wing aircraft, and Grimaldi had been clear from the moment that Bolan leaped into space. Retrieval meant a touchdown, or the next thing to it, during which they would be well in range of any spotter with a rifle or a handgun.

So, no altitude to spare them, and they couldn't count on speed, at least during the pickup.

This time around, Grimaldi would be piloting a Bell ARH-70. The *ARH* stood for Armed Reconnaissance Helicopter—the U.S. Army's replacement for the obsolete OH-58D Kiowa Warrior. His gunship had been painted black, obliterating all insignia and call numbers, but if he got shot down in Pakistan, the hostiles would have no great difficulty calculating where he'd come from.

The solution—don't let any of the bastards shoot you down.

The ARH-70 normally seated a two-man crew, but Grimaldi could fly it alone with no problem. Six passenger seats were four more than he needed for Bolan and guest. The chopper's Honeywell HTS900-2 turboshaft engine let it cruise at 130 mph, with an official top speed of 161 mph, and a maximum range of 186 miles.

The Bell couldn't outrun a bullet or surface-to-air missile, but it wasn't defenseless, either. They called it an armed recon chopper because it packed two deadly punches of its own— a GAU-19 .50-caliber Gatling gun and four pods of Hydra 70 2.75-inch rockets. The Gatling gun fired two thousand rounds per minute, with a killing range of 1,800 meters. The Hydras carried ten-pound high-explosive warheads that would cripple most vehicles and play bloody hell with infantry.

Grimaldi gave himself an hour for the flight across Afghanistan's frontier to Pakistan. He had Bolan's coordinates programmed into the helicopter's GPS system, his only worry now was hostile contact from the ground or in the air.

Pakistan's air force had a mixed combat record prior to 1990, when the U.S. imposed an eleven-year military embargo in response to the country's program of nuclear weapons development. China picked up some of the slack, and the air force now had an estimated five hundred jet fighters— mainly the JF-17 Thunder model, known in its native China as the Chengdu FC-1 Xiaolong.

Some of those would certainly be stationed at Peshawar Airbase, but their threat to Grimaldi and Bolan depended on whether Grimaldi was spotted crossing the border.

The first step toward avoidance would be flying below radar, hugging the deck as best he could from takeoff to his final on-target approach. Beyond that, if Grimaldi felt that he'd been spotted by a military unit while en route to rendezvous, he'd deal with it then, no regrets.

His immediate priority was bringing Bolan out alive. He would accomplish that, regardless of the risks involved, in transit or upon arrival at the landing zone.

And anyone who tried to interfere would pay the price.

THEY LEFT the stolen car two hills away from the selected pickup point and jogged over, still carrying their rifles, handguns and, in Bolan's case, a bandolier of 40 mm rounds for his GP-25 grenade launcher.

They were close to getting out, but you could never be too careful. There was still a chance their enemies would find them, close in for the kill before Grimaldi came to pick them up.

And if he didn't come? Then, what?

It was a possibility, as Bolan realized. Each time the pilot crossed a hostile border without authorization, he risked being shot from the sky by ground troops or the other side's air force. Jack's survival owed almost as much to luck, as skill.

And everybody's luck ran out, sooner or later.

"There should be someone on hand to meet you when we touch down," Bolan told Gorshani, killing time without making it obvious. "If not, I'll wait until they show."

"It feels strange," Gorshani said. "I must leave my home forever, and my last sight of it is these hills."

His eyes scanned slopes with no features of interest, unless he was into dry, brown grass.

"It could be worse," Bolan replied.

"Of course. I simply wondered whether anyone will even notice I am gone."

"The men who want to kill you will," Bolan assured him. "You can reach out to the rest when you get settled on the other side."

"Perhaps," Gorshani said. "But after all the grief I brought down on Sanjrani and my people, maybe it is best that they forget me soon."

"Your call," Bolan said, "but you ought to give them credit where it's due."

"Meaning?"

"They chose to help you, shelter you and keep your secret from the soldiers. That was nothing you forced onto them. Even if you decide to cut them loose, you might want to hang on to that. Remember that they cared."

Gorshani's somber silence stretched into the distance, where a sound intruded on Bolan's consciousness. At first, it was subliminal, almost a feeling, rather than a sound he could interpret and identify. Then, moments later, Bolan had it.

"Here we go," he told Gorshani.

There was still a chance he could be wrong, of course. All helicopters sounded roughly the same, from miles away. This could turn out to be a Pakistani army chopper on patrol, or some kind of commercial flight.

But Bolan didn't think so.

He saw the whirlybird when it was still nearly a mile away. Not clearly, or in detail, but as a speck growing continuously larger in his field of vision, flying low to the horizon. It was painted some dark color—make that black—and sunlight glinted on its windshield.

"Is this your friend?" Gorshani asked.

"Either that," Bolan said, "or the end of the world as we know it."

At two hundred yards he recognized the Bell ARH-70. Not the specific war bird, of course, since its markings were masked and its paint job wasn't army-olive drab, but there was no mistaking the type or the hardware it carried.

Grimaldi circled once around their hilltop, checking the neighborhood for hostiles, then found his mark, hovered a hundred feet above their heads, and settled noisily to earth.

Bolan and Gorshani crouched below the whirling blur of

rotor blades, eyes narrowed to slits in the storm of wind, dust and grass that the chopper whipped into their faces. When Grimaldi got the side door open, the men ran forward, Bolan following Gorshani to prevent a sudden change of heart, and crawled aboard.

A moment later, they were buckled in and rising from the deck, tilting away as Grimaldi turned back in the direction he had come from—toward the frontier of Afghanistan.

Without earphones, there was no hope for conversation. So Bolan settled back and closed his eyes, thankful that he was finished with another mission, that he had survived, and that he'd soon be going home.

Wherever that turned out to be, this week.

He thought about Gorshani for another moment, knowing there was little he could do to smooth the Pakistani's transit from one country to another, but then fatigue stepped up to claim him and sleep carried away every conscious thought.

Nari District, Kunar Province, Afghanistan

TWO VEHICLES STOOD waiting at the landing zone. One was a military Jeep, the other a commercial brand.

The nearest, on Gorshani's left as he disembarked from the black helicopter, was an open-topped military vehicle with three men standing beside it. Two wore jumpsuits and carried pilots' crash helmets, while the third was dressed in ordinary fatigues and a cap.

The second Jeep was a Grand Cherokee, black beneath a heavy layer of road dust. Its driver remained in his seat, door open, his legs dangling outside, his eyes invisible behind mirrored sunglasses.

"Looks like your ride's here," the big American told him, as their pilot joined them on the ground. "Be careful what you let him sell you."

"Yes, I will."

The two pilots approached, nodding to Cooper and the man Gorshani knew only as Jack. Gorshani watched Cooper and Jack move toward the waiting army Jeep, as the new pilots boarded the helicopter for the flight back to who knew where. At first, Gorshani thought that Cooper was deserting him, but then he realized his future was for *him* to choose.

"Matt!"

Gorshani reached him as the tall American was shedding weapons, stacking them in the back of the small open Jeep. He thought that Cooper looked quite different, without guns, grenades and knives strapped all over his body.

Still, when he looked into the man's eyes, there was a silent darkness lurking that would never be mistaken for benevolence.

"I wish to thank you now, while there is time," Gorshani said. "For everything."

"Hey, *you* helped *me*."

"I think you understand me," he replied.

The soldier held his eyes, then nodded.

"Yes, I do."

They shook hands, then Gorshani turned to Grimaldi, thanked him and turned away to meet the stranger who now stood beside his dusty black Jeep, waiting.

"Mr. Gorshani," the stranger said, as Gorshani joined him. "Or is it Hussein? It wouldn't be the first time someone bitched the paperwork."

"Hussein Gorshani."

"Right. Okay. Ready to take a ride?"

Gorshani hesitated, standing by his open door.

"What about this?" he asked the driver, holding up his rifle.

"Toss it in the back, together with whatever else you're carrying. I've got a blanket on the floor, back there, to cover up. Someone will ditch it later, maybe send it back with interest to the other side."

"What if we're stopped?" Gorshani asked.

"No sweat," the stranger told him. "Diplomatic plates."

Gorshani placed his weapons on the rear floorboards and covered them, then slid into the shotgun seat and closed his door. The Jeep was new and still smelled it, despite the hot day and its heavy layer of dust.

Through tinted glass, he saw the army Jeep already off and rolling, but a dust swirl from the helicopter's lift-off blurred Gorshani's vision. He could not tell whether Cooper or the pilot looked in his direction as they left.

"So, did you have a good flight in?" Gorshani's driver asked him. "I guess that's a stupid question, eh?"

Gorshani shrugged, unwilling to insult the man before he even knew his name.

As if reading his mind, the stranger said, "I'm Jack Armstrong, in case you're wondering. At least, I am today." He smiled at his own joke. "This time tomorrow, hey! Who knows?"

"You represent Central Intelligence?" Gorshani asked.

"Hey, ouch! We don't say that out loud, okay? Not outside Langley, anyway. It's just the Company."

"Of course."

Jack Armstrong revved the Grand Cherokee's engine, put it in gear and followed the dust plume of Matt Cooper's dwindling Jeep.

"We've got a couple hours on the road," said Armstrong, still wearing his cocky smile. "Why don't we talk about your future, eh? I've got some opportunities you may want to consider. Hell, you play your cards right, we might even find a way to send you home eventually."

Arlington National Cemetery

THE ROUND BLACK SIGN read Silence and Respect. Beyond it, more than 290,000 white markers stood in neatly ordered rows, stretching as far as eyes could see across 640 acres.

The road from Arlington's entrance, called Memorial Drive, ran across the Potomac River to the Lincoln Memorial in Washington, linking the giant statue of America's sixteenth president to the cemetery established in June 1864, ten months before an assassin's point-blank pistol killed Abraham Lincoln.

Bolan was not averse to following that road or driving through the capital where he had once been hunted by a small army of law-enforcement officers. The meet at Arlington was Hal Brognola's choice.

Bolan suspected that his old friend liked to stand among the fallen heroes while they talked, because it helped remind him of their reasons for pursuing what both recognized as war everlasting. The men and women buried here had given everything they had.

Bolan and Brognola could do no less.

He saw Brognola coming from a hundred yards away, his snap-brim hat almost an artifact from bygone days. The big Fed took his time, first scanning markers, then homing in on Bolan's figure with determined strides. No one who saw him—if they had been close enough—would have taken him for a common tourist.

"So," Brognola said, when he was close enough to reach for Bolan's hand. "You've kept up with the news, I guess."

A nod from Bolan. It was hard to miss the stories coming from Islamabad, spun first by PTV News to give the story a pro-government slant, then snatched from the airwaves and tweaked by Western news outlets, hammered by pundits of the right and left, finally driven into the ground by late-night comedians.

In broad strokes, Pakistan's leaders had first stalled for time, then announced their "heroic" defeat of an al Qaeda faction led by none other than Akram Ben Abd al-Bari, the second-most wanted fugitive terrorist on Earth. Al-Bari and his followers had died, along with an uncertain number of Pakistani soldiers and civilians.

"No diplomatic rumbles, then?" he asked Brognola.

Brognola frowned, mock-concentrating. "There was something," he replied, stretching the words out. "Oh, right. Our embassy in Kabul got a vague protest about violations of Pakistani airspace. It sounded serious, but there were no specifics as to type of aircraft or what have you. I suppose the consul's office round-filed it."

"Jack's very smooth," Bolan said.

"Jack?" Brognola cocked a brow. "Who's Jack?"

They strolled past markers dating from what *Time* magazine had called "the Last Good War." Bolan knew what the writers had in mind, but having fought his share of wars—and then some—he could say with certainty that none were good.

Perhaps good came from some of them. But he'd leave that judgment to the historians.

"No word about Gorshani, I suppose?"

Brognola paused before a snow-white Star of David, flanked by crosses.

"None expected, none received," he said. "You left him with a fellow from the Company, I take it?"

"Right."

"Well, there you are then. Flip a coin."

Meaning that it was fifty-fifty whether Langley would reward Gorshani for his service to the cause or try to use him yet again. And it was always possible, of course, that they would simply cut him loose, perhaps with severance pay, a handshake and a solemn "Don't call us."

Brognola broke in on his thoughts, saying, "You did some good, the two of you. Hell, *you* know that, of all people."

"It wasn't his choice, though," Bolan replied. "Pulling up roots, I mean. He didn't see that coming."

"Then he wasn't looking far enough ahead," Brognola said. "You need to think about the long view, even if you can't see past the next ten seconds."

Bolan nodded once again, acceptance of the truth that had

defined his life since he'd first donned a uniform, and then after he'd discarded it.

"Too bad, though," Bolan said.

"Maybe he'll have a happy ending."

"Maybe."

"Anyway," Brognola said, "another job's come up. We ought to talk about it."

"So, let's talk," Bolan replied.

He kept pace with his oldest living friend, among the ranks of graves.

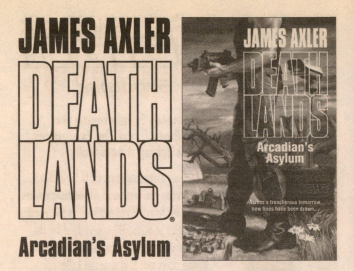

James Axler
Outlanders®

INFINITY BREACH

An open door to the heart of the cosmos heralds unearthly danger...

In the secret Arctic laboratory of a brilliant twentieth-century adventurer, an Annunaki artifact of staggering power rips a portal deep into time and space. Emerging from the breach, breathtaking beings of Light appear like antibodies to close the rupture. But these wondrous Angels have their own solution to healing the infinity breach—the complete eradication of mankind!

Available May 2010 wherever books are sold.